Annabella f   *th, inhaled his special aroma. She was conscious of every inch of her own body as well as Terry's.*

"Tell me, Miss Annabella Abraham," Terry said, turning her to face him. He wrapped his fingers around the wavy cascade of her hair, drawing her near with gentle pulling. "If I were to kiss you under this big oak tree in the moonlight, would you punch me in the eye?"

"No," she said, her voice hushed.

"I'm glad to hear it." Terry needed no more invitation than that. The kiss was long and powerful, sensuous and sweet, give and take. It was heat. Desire. Bodies yearning to savor, taste, all there was. The kiss was passion rising, breathing becoming rough, hearts beating wildly. The kiss was want. It was the promise of more, of what might be, should their hearts and minds consent. . . .

WHAT ARE *LOVESWEPT* ROMANCES?

They are stories of true romance and touching emotion. We believe those two very important ingredients are constants in our highly sensual and very believable stories in the *LOVESWEPT* line. Our goal is to give you, the reader, stories of consistently high quality that may sometimes make you laugh, sometimes make you cry, but are always fresh and creative and contain many delightful surprises within their pages.

Most romance fans read an enormous number of books. Those they truly love, they keep. Others may be traded with friends and soon forgotten. We hope that each *LOVESWEPT* romance will be a treasure—a "keeper." We will always try to publish

LOVE STORIES YOU'LL NEVER FORGET
BY AUTHORS YOU'LL ALWAYS REMEMBER

The Editors

LOVESWEPT® • 265

Joan Elliott Pickart
The Enchanting
Miss Annabella

BANTAM BOOKS
TORONTO • NEW YORK • LONDON • SYDNEY • AUCKLAND

For Sharon and Lorraine

THE ENCHANTING MISS ANNABELLA

A Bantam Book / July 1988

*LOVESWEPT® and the wave device are registered
trademarks of Bantam Books, a division of
Bantam Doubleday Dell Publishing Group, Inc.
Registered in U.S. Patent
and Trademark Office and elsewhere.*

*If you would be interested in receiving protective vinyl
covers for your Loveswept books, please write to this address
for information:*

> Loveswept
> Bantam Books
> P.O. Box 985
> Hicksville, NY 11802

ISBN 0-553-21908-1

Published simultaneously in the United States and Canada

*Bantam Books are published by Bantam Books, a division
of Bantam Doubleday Dell Publishing Group, Inc. Its trademark, consisting of the words "Bantam Books" and the
portrayal of a rooster, is Registered in U.S. Patent and
Trademark Office and in other countries. Marca Registrada.
Bantam Books, 666 Fifth Avenue, New York, New York 10103.*

PRINTED IN THE UNITED STATES OF AMERICA

O   0 9 8 7 6 5 4 3 2 1

One

Terry Russell heard a deep groan of pleasure, and absently realized it had rumbled up from his own chest and escaped from his own lips. It was the sound made by a man experiencing ecstasy in its purest form, and he was neither surprised nor embarrassed that the groan had come from him.

She was sleek and beautiful, he thought. She responded to his hands as though custom-made just for him: Lifting, turning. She did whatever he asked of her. If he were to die at that moment, it would be with a smile on his face.

But he wasn't going to die, he knew, because she was perfect. She'd take him as high as he wanted to go, soaring. She'd give him all he asked of her without a whisper of complaint, and he'd reward her with his expertise and the knowing touch of his gentle hands. She purred for him, she sang for him, her energy and power under his command.

Higher . . . the heavens . . . as one.

Then down, down, oh, so slowly, savoring it all, relishing the sensations, returning to reality reluctantly.

Terry sighed, a satisfied, appreciative sigh for what she had given him, how she had made him feel.

She was, Terry thought, one of the finest little Cessna two-seater airplanes he'd ever flown.

"You're a real honey, sweetheart," he said as he approached the runway. "I could have stayed up there with you all day."

The wheels touched down with a soft bump, then Terry slowly taxied toward the small building, delaying the moment when he would have to relinquish his claim on the lovely lady who was still responding like a dream to his masterful hands.

Annabella Abraham had lost the feeling in her fingers from clenching her hands so tightly. She had also closed her eyes, because her stomach had lurched up, then down, matching each motion of the small white plane in the sky she'd been watching. Only now did she cautiously open one eye and peer across the tarmac to see if the plane had landed safely.

"Oh, praise be," she murmured, opening her other eye, "the idiot is back on the ground."

While Annabella Abraham had no idea who was piloting the plane, she automatically put him into the category of those unfortunate souls who do not possess their full mental faculties. She was a firm believer in the old adage that if God had meant man to fly, the human race would have been born with wings. It was a sensible philosophy. She kept it tucked in her mind next to the adage that says if man were meant to swim, he'd have fins, or flippers, or gills, or whatever.

No, Annabella thought as she pried her fingers apart. No sane person climbed into one of those airplanes and took off into the heavens with nothing more solid between him and death but air and a marshmallow cloud or two.

But, she admitted, the even more insane fact to be dealt with at the moment was that the airplane making its way slowly toward her belonged to her! She, Annabella Abraham, actually owned the horrendous thing. And she had absolutely no idea what she was going to do with it.

Annabella watched as the plane stopped. A few minutes later a small door opened and a tall man ducked his head and stepped out onto the wing. In one smooth, graceful motion he swung to the ground and began to stride forward.

Standing in the shadows of the building, Annabella scrutinized the pilot, the totally insane man, who had just risked life and limb to fly that ridiculous machine. He came closer, covering the hot concrete quickly with long legs clad in very tight faded jeans.

He didn't look insane, Annabella conceded. He appeared to be an ordinary man. Well, no, that wasn't quite true either. There was nothing ordinary about the width of those shoulders or the way his blue T-shirt stretched across his broad chest and hugged his flat stomach. And it was quite extraordinary, really, how the sun transformed his thick blond hair into a glowing halo. He was very tall and very tan, and—no, not ordinary at all.

The door of the whitewashed wooden building was flung open, and a short, round man, whom Annabella knew to be Barney Chisholm, bustled out.

"Well?" Barney asked. "Is she a beauty or what, Terry?"

Terry, Annabella mused. That was an ordinary name. Nice, but ordinary.

"Barney," Terry said, clapping the older man on the shoulder, "I owe you one. That plane is a honey, responded to my touch like a willing woman."

Well! Really! Annabella thought indignantly. A willing woman, indeed.

"I knew you'd be in seventh heaven, boy," Barney said. "That's why I called you to come out here. The pilot who flew her up from Tulsa is inside waiting for you to sign the papers saying he delivered her in A-OK condition. He wants to hit the road."

"You bet," Terry said. "Did I hear you right on the phone? This sweet baby belongs to some old maid librarian here in Harmony?"

Annabella fumed. She was twenty-nine years old, and by today's standards that did not place her in the category of old maid. She was a . . . career woman. Yes, exactly. She was dedicated to her career.

"It's a fact," Barney said. "Miss Annabella won the plane in one of them raffles at an opening of a new grocery store in Tulsa. Isn't that the craziest thing you ever heard? She's supposed to be out here to sign for it, but I haven't seen her yet."

That was typical, Annabella thought, sighing inwardly. It was always like that. No one ever seemed to see her, even though she might be nearly standing under his nose. All of her life she'd just seemed to fade into the woodwork.

"Well, I'll sign the papers," Terry said, "so the pilot can be on his way." He glanced up. "Who's that?"

Barney turned. "Oh, there's Miss Annabella. She must have just got here. Come on, I'll introduce you. She's only been in Harmony 'bout three years. It's been more than that since you've been home, boy. You're overdue for a visit, that's for sure."

Annabella lifted her chin and prepared herself to meet the lunatic named Terry. He was suddenly right in front of her, and she tipped her head back to look up at him.

Oh, merciful saints, she thought, those blue eyes were *not* ordinary. Never had she seen such eyes on such a handsome face. He was smiling at her? Gracious, what a smile, what a butter-melting smile.

"Miss Annabella Abraham," Barney said, "this is Terry Russell. Terry, this is Miss Annabella, the librarian, and the owner of the plane."

"Ma'am," Terry said, extending his hand.

Annabella looked at his hand, his smiling face, then his hand again. Finally she lifted her own hand and placed it in his, immediately feeling the long length of his fingers curl around her smaller ones.

A bird, Terry thought suddenly. She reminded him of a small brown sparrow. She had brown hair pulled into a tight bun at her neck, enormous brown eyes, and was wearing a brown dress and shoes. A fragile, little brown sparrow. She wasn't unattractive, but then again she wasn't pretty, she was just . . . there.

"Mr. Russell," Annabella said, inclining her head. She slowly retrieved her hand.

Holy hell, Terry thought, stiffening. *That* voice had come out of *that* little sparrow? He felt as though he'd been punched in the gut. Her voice was low and soft, his own name seeming to flow over him like . . . like brown velvet. Lord, what a voice.

"Terry grew up in Harmony, Miss Annabella," Barney said. "Raised hell as a kid. His folks are still here, retired now, and Terry flies for a big, fancy outfit in New York City. He's home visiting his folks for a spell. I remember the time—"

"Barney," Terry said, "let's get those papers signed, shall we? That pilot from Tulsa is eager to go, and I imagine Miss Annabella is getting warm standing out here in the sun."

"Oh, well, yes," Barney said. "Let's us all go on inside."

"Ma'am," Terry said. He flashed her a dazzling smile and indicated the door with a sweep of his arm.

Annabella nodded politely and turned to enter the building.

Damn, Terry thought, following close on her heels. She hadn't said anything. He wanted to hear her voice again; he wanted to learn if it were true or he had only imagined that Miss Annabella Abraham, librarian, had the most sexy, sultry, sensuous voice he'd ever heard. He'd probably imagined it. Plain, little brown sparrows did not have voices like that!

Inside the building Terry signed the release for the pilot from Tulsa, and Annabella added her signature to the form in the designated place with a trembling hand. The two men chatted a moment about the merits of the Cessna, then the pilot left, saying he had a friend waiting outside to drive him back to Tulsa.

The telephone rang in a nearby office, and Barney lumbered off, muttering under his breath about a man never having a moment's peace.

Terry leaned back against the counter, crossed one ankle over the other, and folded his arms loosely across his chest. He looked hard at Annabella Abraham.

"So," he said, "it would seem that you own an airplane."

"So it would seem," she said, then sighed.

There it was . . . that voice. He hadn't imagined it at all. Incredible, Terry thought. Absolutely incredible. Actually, now that he really looked at her, she wasn't all that bad. Taken individually, her features were lovely—big brown eyes, a cute little nose with a dab of freckles, and pretty lips, very nice lips. She didn't wear a speck of makeup, not even lipstick or lip gloss, or whatever women called it. Her face was really pretty, he mused. It was just that the overall picture of her was drab, dull. But, holy smoke, that voice!

"What do you plan to do with the plane?" Terry asked.

"I don't know," she said, throwing up her hands. "I tried to tell the people running the raffle that I didn't want it, but they said I had to accept it. Oh, I wish I'd never put the ticket in the barrel for the drawing. I've never in my life taken a chance on anything. And now I have to pay taxes on that . . . that thing and . . . oh, dear."

Terry thought he might do something he'd regret because every sexy, sultry word she'd spoken had landed with a heated thud low, very low, in his body. A coiled ache lodged there and inspired him to think of ways to keep her talking for the next twenty-four hours straight.

"Well," he asked, "did you ever consider the possibility of taking flying lessons and enjoying your prize?"

Annabella's eyes grew even bigger, and she placed her hand over her heart. "Oh, no. My goodness, no. I'd be terrified. I've never flown, never. Just watching you while you were up there doing all those fancy loops, and ups and downs, was enough to give me a fright. Oh, no, I could never fly that awful thing."

Terry straightened and shifted his weight to reach out and lightly grip her shoulders. "Hey, relax," he said gently. "You're white as a ghost. It was just a suggestion. Forget I even mentioned it." She looked so frightened, and he wanted to haul her into his arms and comfort her, tell her to push from her mind any thought of going up in that plane, tell her that nothing would hurt her because he was there. "Okay?"

Heat, Annabella thought. There was such heat in Terry Russell's large hands. Heat that was traveling down her arms and across her breasts, causing her breasts to feel strange, heavy, achy.

"Miss Annabella, are you all right?" Terry asked.

"What? Oh, yes, of course." She stepped out of his

grasp, and instantly missed the heat from his big hands. "I'm terribly sorry, Mr. Russell. I overreacted. It's just that I have a fear of flying, and this whole business of winning an airplane has been unsettling, to say the least."

He smiled. "Yes, I can see that."

"Second prize in the drawing was a lovely set of china with violets on the border. It was the sight of those pretty dishes that prompted me to fill out the coupon. It was a foolish thing to do."

"Not if you like pretty dishes with violets," he said. "I wish you had won them."

"So do I." She glanced out the window. "What am I going to do with that airplane? I have to pay Mr. Chisholm rent hangar space—I think that's what he called it—and then there's the taxes. . . ."

"Look, I know a lot of pilots all over the country. Would you like me to check around, see if anyone would be interested in buying it?"

"Would you?"

"Sure. The plane isn't new, you know. It's a 1985 Cessna 152. That was the last year that Cessna made a two-seater model. I'd guess that the big shots of the grocery store chain used it for company business, then donated it for the drawing."

"I suppose they told me," she said, "but I was so flustered I didn't remember a word."

"Well, it hasn't had much use. It flies like a dream. You'll have to understand, though, that a potential buyer is going to want the price dropped quite a bit because of its age, whether it's in prime condition or not."

"That's fine, just fine," Annabella said quickly.

"I'm not concerned about how much money I get for it as long as I no longer own it."

"Then I'll do my best to sell the plane for you, Miss Annabella."

"I would be very grateful if you could, Mr. Russell."

And then Miss Annabella Abraham smiled.

"Oh-h-h . . . Lord," Terry said under his breath.

Blood pounded through his veins as he stared at Annabella, seeing the transformation that came over her face. She had straight, white teeth and a dimple in her right cheek, and a sparkle suddenly shone in the depths of her big brown eyes.

How, Terry wondered, had he ever chalked this woman up as plain, dull, drab? That smile, on that face, combined with that voice, were turning him inside out.

"How can I ever thank you?" Annabella asked.

He could definitely think of a way, Terry thought dryly. If she knew how much heated pressure was building within him, she'd probably faint dead away. He'd never want her to fall flat on her pretty little freckled nose, he realized wistfully.

"No problem," he said. "I can't guarantee anything, though."

"I know, but just the fact that you're trying will make me feel immensely better."

Immensely better? Terry mentally repeated. Wouldn't she feel a "helluva lot" better? No. Miss Annabella wouldn't dream of saying such a thing. She was like a woman of another era who had stepped through a looking glass into the wrong time zone. She was out of place even in a small, laid-back town like Harmony, Oklahoma. She even had *him* thinking of her as Miss Annabella instead of just Ann, or Anna, or Annie, or—

"Well, I must be going," Annabella said. "It was a pleasure meeting you, Mr. Russell."

"Terry."

"Pardon me?"

"Call me Terry, and I'll call you . . . um—" ah, hell—"Miss Annabella," he finished, with a shrug.

"Oh, well, all right . . . Terry. Oh, dear, I don't suppose I can just leave that plane sitting there, can I? It belongs in its garage or hangar or whatever."

"I'll take care of it," Terry said.

"Thank you. Goodness, I do seem to thank you a great deal, don't I? I'm just so appreciative of your assistance."

He grinned. "I don't think anyone has ever been appreciative of my assistance before. You do have a way with words, Miss Annabella."

"I do?" she asked, appearing surprised. "What a lovely compliment. Well, good day, Mr. . . . Terry."

"Yeah. See ya," he said. He watched her walk toward the door. "Hold it," he said, striding to stand in front of her again. "I need your phone number and address. You know, so I can keep in touch with you about my progress on selling the plane. Are you in the phone book?"

"Yes."

"Great. Fine. I'll be talking to you then. Bye." He looked directly into her eyes, and his heart thudded like a bongo drum in his chest.

He really did have beautiful blue eyes, Annabella mused. They matched the T-shirt he wore. They matched the sky where she'd watched him fly her plane. Was she staring, gawking at his eyes? Merciful saints, she was! How absolutely mortifying.

"Good day again," she said, then hurried out the door.

"Yes," he said softly.

Mesmerized, Terry stood by the door watching Annabella walk over and get into a metallic gray compact car. He didn't move as she drove away, leaving behind a trail of dust. And still he didn't move as the image of Miss Annabella Abraham played through his mind. He tried to find a slot to put her in. But she didn't fit anywhere because she was like no woman he had ever met.

She was old-fashioned, he thought, but there was more to her than that. Her voice alone conjured up scenarios of bedrooms and lovemaking, hours and hours of lovemaking. And her smile? Lord, that smile. It had thrown his libido for a real loop. She was an enigma, Miss Annabella Abraham. Indeed she was.

"Terry?" Barney said, coming out of his office. "Oh, there you are. Another lost package, and everyone is in a flap. Hell, I don't have the damned thing. Did Miss Annabella leave?"

"Yeah, I said I'd see that the plane got in the hangar."

"Put it in hangar two. The roof is leaking in three."

"Okay. Barney, just who is Annabella Abraham?"

"The librarian."

"So you said. But where did she come from?" he asked. *The Twilight Zone*, he immediately thought, then chided himself.

"Do you remember old Bessie Montgomery? She

taught school here for what seemed like a hundred years."

"Sure, I remember her."

"Well, she passed on a few years back. About three years, I guess, 'cause that's how long Miss Annabella has been here. Bessie was her aunt, left her a little house on Peach Street. Miss Annabella came for the funeral and stayed on. We're mighty pleased to have her at the library. She's fixed things up nice, the way they had 'em in the library in Tulsa where she worked before. Heard her say once that she's never been out of the state of Oklahoma. Don't surprise me none. She wouldn't be brave enough to travel. She's scared of her own shadow, seems to me. But everyone likes Miss Annabella."

"Does she . . . you know, date? Go out with anyone?"

"Not that I heard tell of. There's twitters about Ralph Newberry spending a mighty lot of time in the library lately, but I don't think he's asked her out. Ralph's scared of his own shadow, too." Barney laughed. "They'd make a great pair."

"Hell, Ralph is nearly fifty years old."

"Guess he is at that. Time sure does fly by. Miss Annabella is twenty-nine."

"Oh? How do you know?"

"Emily Engels mentioned it at bingo. Emily sends in the applications for renewing drivers' licenses. She saw Miss Annabella's birth date on the form."

Terry laughed. "This town hasn't changed a bit. Everybody knows everybody's business."

"That's the truth."

"I'll put the Cessna in the hangar, Barney."

"Fine. Good to see you, Terry. You sure do know how to handle an airplane. Like a willing woman, you said. Loved the way you put that. Give my best to your folks."

"Will do. See ya," Terry said.

He left the building and walked slowly toward the gleaming white plane. A willing woman, he repeated to himself. He'd handled his share. He flew all over the world in the company jet for St. John Enterprises and knew a lot of willing women in every shape and size.

But how, he wondered, did a guy handle an un-willing woman? An old-fashioned, not-of-this-world, *Twilight Zone* woman like Miss Annabella Abraham? Hell, forget handle. What did a guy even *say* to a woman like her? But an even better question was, why was he worried about it? She sure as hell wasn't his type.

Terry stopped beside the plane and slid his glance over the sleek aircraft, nodding in approval. He smiled as he recalled Annabella's saying she'd much rather have had the pretty dishes with the violets on them.

She was something, all right, Terry mused. But what exactly she was, he wasn't sure. All he really knew for certain at this point was that she had a knockout smile and a voice that made his blood run hot. She was full of surprises, and he might just decide to discover what else was hidden beneath the surface of the pretty little sparrow.

Terry swung up onto the wing of the plane and entered through the small door. He was whistling.

• • •

Arriving back in town from the airport, Annabella went directly to the grocery store to do her Saturday shopping. Her purchases were basically the same each week: fresh fruit and vegetables, fish, poultry, rice and potatoes, any ingredients she might need to bake her own bread and make sugar tea-cookies. She replenished her cleaning supplies if need be and always made sure she had plenty of spiced-apple tea. She knew where everything was located in the store and always placed her items in her cart in the same precise order.

Today she entered the small store rather cautiously, still remembering with a flush of embarrassment how everyone had gathered around her the previous week. The news of her winning the airplane had been in the morning paper, and the people of Harmony, Oklahoma, had been in an excited dither.

Having no idea what to say to the chattering group that had descended upon her, Annabella had finally edged away. To her profound relief no one had seemed to notice her absence, and she'd proceeded with her shopping. The others had simply continued talking about how marvelous it would be to win such a fabulous prize. Her nerves had been so jangled, however, she'd totally forgotten to purchase her spiced-apple tea. Rather than return and possibly face more questions, she'd reused the same tea bag for the past two days, hoping this week's trip to the grocery store would be uneventful.

Through the week she had managed to avoid discussing the airplane at the library by bustling around and appearing ever-so-very busy at all times. Her part-time assistant, elderly Mrs. Perdy, was more interested in talking about her soap operas than that "fancy, fandangled airplane you won yourself, Miss Annabella."

In the store Annabella glanced quickly around, grabbed a shopping cart, and made a beeline for the produce section. Two plums, two peaches, two bananas, two apples went into Annabella's cart. Those were followed by two carrots, two ears of corn, and a small bunch of fresh broccoli. She was examining a rather scrawny cucumber when she heard voices behind her.

"Hi, Susie, how are the kids?" a woman asked.

"Ornery. I swear, they have Jack's personality— crabby. Say, did you hear? Terry Russell is home visiting his folks. Oh, I can still remember going into a swoon when he passed me in the hall in high school. You had a crush on him, too, Clara."

Annabella peered more closely at the cucumber.

"Didn't we all?" Clara asked, laughing. "Margaret saw him yesterday afternoon. She called me and said that Terry is even better-looking than ever. She said the older he gets, the yummier he gets."

Yummier? Annabella asked herself. Was that a word?

"No kidding? Let's see, he must be about thirty-six now," Susie said. "I wonder if he'll ever remarry?"

Remarry? Annabella thought, staring at the cucumber. As in, do it again because he'd already done it once before? Terry Russell was divorced?

"I don't know," Clara said. "Misty died well over nine years ago now. I think that if Terry was going to remarry he would have done it already. Heavens, he lives in New York, flies all over the world for that

big, important company he works for. I imagine he
has his pick of glamorous women."

Terry's wife had died? Annabella thought, squeez-
ing the cucumber. How terribly sad. How terribly,
terribly sad.

"Margaret said," Clara went on, with a giggle, "that
after she saw him yesterday, she fantasized for an
hour about what it would be like to make love with
him. She says he's built like a dream."

Oh, merciful saints, Annabella thought, gripping
the cucumber with both hands. How could two
women, wives and mothers, discuss such things in
the produce department?

"A little daydreaming never hurt anyone," Susie
said. "If I were married to Margaret's Henry, I'd fantasize, too."

"I'm with you," Clara said. "I read in a maga-
zine that romantic fantasizing is very healthy for a
woman."

Really? Annabella thought. She'd never read that
anywhere. Romantic fantasizing. How did one go
about doing such a thing? Forget it, she told herself. It was absurd.

Susie laughed. "Well, maybe I'll see Terry and fantasize a dab myself."

"Oh, me, too," Clara said. "I'll picture taking off
Terry Russell's clothes piece by piece, then I'll—"
Annabella broke the cucumber in half, then stared
at it in wide-eyed horror— "touch him," Clara rambled on, a dreamy quality to her voice. "And kiss
him, and . . . oh, darn, look at the time. I have to
get Davy to the dentist. Talk to you soon, Susie."

"See you, Clara. I have to rush too."

Annabella peeked over her shoulder to see the two women disappear in opposite directions. She switched her gaze back to the demolished cucumber in her hands, then with a defeated sigh placed both halves in a plastic bag and secured it with a blue twisty-tie. She tossed it into her cart and didn't even care when it landed with a thud on top of her peaches.

Annabella whipped her cart around and shut out thoughts of anything except grocery shopping. She whizzed through the store with a speed that would have shocked and amazed anyone who'd noticed. But no one noticed Annabella Abraham.

She drove to her small, two-bedroom, redbrick house on Peach Street with the perfectly manicured postage-stamp-size front lawn and the row of red geraniums in front of the porch. She carried in her groceries and put everything away in its proper place, ignoring for the moment the bruised peaches and broken cucumber. At last she settled into her rocker in the living room with a cup of spiced-apple tea, brewed with a fresh bag.

Then, and only then, did she think.

Then, and only then, did she think about Terry Russell. Tall, tanned, blond, smiling Terry Russell. Terry, who had lost his young wife years before. Terry, who caused respectable wives and mothers of Harmony, Oklahoma, to have romantic fantasies. Take off his clothes piece by piece and . . .? Merciful saints.

Romantic fantasies? Annabella mused on. They were healthy for a woman to have? Whatever for? After all, what was the point of daydreaming about taking off Terry's clothes? It would be much more practical to have the man actually there in person and *really* take off his clothes.

"Annabella!" she said, stiffening in her chair and nearly spilling her tea. She'd never entertained such wanton mental wanderings in her life. Imagine sitting in her own living room deciding on the most efficient way to rid Terry Russell of his clothes. Shame on her.

It was the airplane, Annabella decided. She hadn't been herself since coming face to face with that frightful machine. Her jangled nerves had nothing to do with Terry, it was that plane. Well, her tea would calm her down and she'd be fine. Besides, Terry was going to help her get rid of the gruesome machine, and her life would get back to normal. Splendid.

Annabella frowned, rocking slowly as she sipped her tea. Her life would get back to normal? Would she do the same thing day in day out, week after week, month after month, she asked herself. Well, of course, she would. She'd established a very pleasing pattern for her life. She liked Harmony, the people, her little house, her job at the library. She belonged to the Quilting Club and contributed to all the bake sales at the church, having established a reputation for making delicious bread and sugar tea-cookies. She had an endless, wonderful supply of books to read from the library. . . .

But she'd never, ever, read that it was healthy for a woman to have romantic fantasies.

Did that mean, Annabella pondered, that it was rather unhealthy from a mental standpoint if a woman *didn't* indulge in such things? No, surely not. For the life of her she couldn't see what purpose such fantasies would serve.

Annabella set her cup and saucer on the polished end table, rested her elbow on the arm of the chair, and propped her chin in her hand. She continued to rock.

Maybe she should think this through, she decided. There was no point in fantasizing about being kissed, as she'd had that experience several times when she'd dated on occasion when she'd lived in Tulsa. A kiss was . . . a kiss. It certainly wasn't an earth-shattering event.

But then again . . . What if one were kissed by a man like Terry Russell?

Somehow, she knew, Terry's kiss just might move the earth. She'd never met a man like Terry before. She'd never felt such strange heat course through her body as when he'd placed his strong hands on her shoulders. Had never seen such beautiful blue eyes on a face that was handsome beyond belief or a smile that seemed capable of dissolving her bones. Yes, a kiss shared with Terry could very well be an earth-shattering event.

He would lean toward her, his breath warm and sweet as it fluttered over her skin. Then his sensuous lips would claim hers and—

"Oh, mercy," Annabella said, her hands flying to her flushed cheeks. She was doing it! She was engaging in a romantic fantasy! How awful. How embarrassing. How . . . tingly she felt inside, how aware of every inch of her own body. Her breasts were heavy, achy, just as they'd been when Terry's hands had gripped her shoulders. This wasn't healthy, it was frightening!

Annabella got to her feet and returned the cup and saucer to the kitchen. She went into her bedroom, which had white eyelet curtains at the window and a spread on the double bed of a fabric sprigged with delicate violets.

She caught a glimpse of her reflection as she passed the full-length mirror on the wall, and stopped, turning to view herself.

There she was, she thought dryly, Annabella Abraham. She'd looked the same for just about as long as she could remember. She was five feet five and weighed exactly one hundred and twelve pounds. She had long legs, slender hips, and breasts much too large for the rest of her borderline skinny self. She wore loose-fitting clothes in conservative colors to camouflage her disaster of a figure and chose sensible shoes to perform her job more efficiently at the library. Yes, for what it was worth, there she was.

On impulse Annabella reached up and drew the pins from the bun at the nape of her neck. Her heavy, wavy hair tumbled halfway down her back, and she pulled it forward to fall over her breasts . . . breasts that still ached from the remembrance of the strong, heated touch of Terry Russell's hands on her shoulders.

Two

Terry sat on the screened porch on the back of his parents' home and watched the fireflies dancing through the summer night. He'd spent the afternoon helping his father remove a tree stump from the side yard and was pleasantly tired. He sat on an old wooden swing suspended from the ceiling by chains and pushed it slowly back and forth with one foot, his other leg propped at the ankle on his knee. His father, Mike, sat in a recliner, the aroma of his favorite pipe tobacco wafting through the air.

Memories of his youth, of growing up in that house with his parents and sisters, crept in around Terry like the familiar fragrance of his father's tobacco.

It was great to be home, he mused. He could feel himself starting to unwind, to come down from the high-speed chase his life had become as he flew the St. John Enterprises' private jet from one place to the next. He liked his job, the people he worked with, and especially the flying. But now, at that moment, it was great to be home.

Mary Russell came out onto the porch carrying a tray with three tall glasses of lemonade.

"Thanks, Mom," Terry said, taking a glass. "I was just sitting here going down memory lane and had decided that the only thing missing was your lemonade made from the lemons on that tree over there." He took a deep swallow. "Perfect."

Mary handed Mike a glass, then settled with her own on a cushioned chair. "It's good to have you home, Terry," she said. "And, yes, this does bring back memories of summers in the past, doesn't it?"

Mike Russell chuckled. "Depends on how far back you're going. If it was when all three of the kids were still home, you'd be hearing the girls hollering at Terry to leave them alone so they could get ready for their dates. And they'd be saying, if Terry said one thing to the heartthrobs of the hour, they'd drown him in the bathtub."

"They picked on me," Terry said with a smile. "I was the best little brother any two sisters could have asked for, but they never appreciated me."

"Oh, you were a handful," Mary said, with a soft laugh.

"I was innovative, Mother. I kept everyone on his toes."

"Now, that's a fact," Mike said.

"Well, it's worth saying again that it's good to have you here," Mary said. "I know we've all been together at Christmas the past few years at your sisters' homes in Detroit or Miami, but it has been so long since I've had you under this roof, sleeping in your own bed, feeding you good, healthy food, and—"

"Making outstanding lemonade," Terry said, then drained his glass. "It's great to be here, Mom. I was more tired than I realized. I knew I needed a vacation, though, when I got off the St. John Enterprises' jet in Paris and couldn't remember what city I was in."

His mother clicked her tongue. "You work too hard."

"Everyone does at times," Terry said. "I can remember Dad dragging home bone weary from the garage. It happens. Do you miss it, Dad?"

"The garage? No, I was ready to retire. I wander down there sometimes and they put me to work troubleshooting an engine or changing spark plugs. That's enough for me." He paused. "I imagine that's a honey of an engine in that Cessna Miss Annabella won."

Terry swooped his hand through the air in a smooth motion. "It purrs," he said. "It moved under my touch like a willing—" he glanced quickly at his mother—"airplane."

Mike chuckled and Terry shot him a quick grin.

"Imagine Miss Annabella owning an airplane," Mary said, oblivious of the men's joke. "That dear little girl must be all in a dither."

"She's not the least bit happy about it," Terry said. "She would rather have won the china dishes with the violets on the border."

"That sounds like Miss Annabella," Mike said. "Sometimes she reminds me of a timid mouse."

A little sparrow, Terry thought. Who was afraid to

fly. Not only afraid to fly in airplanes, but too frightened, perhaps, to try her wings at life. Ah-h-h, he was being a poetic pilot. He was a great poetic pilot at times.

"Well," Terry said, "I told her I'd check around and see if I could sell the plane for her. That seemed to calm her down."

"It's very thoughtful of you to try and sell the plane for Miss Annabella, Terry," Mary said.

"I'll see what I can do. Why does everyone call her Miss Annabella? Even you two do it, and she's only twenty-nine."

"I never thought about it," Mike said. "Everyone calls her that. Seems proper, somehow. Miss Annabella isn't like the other young people around. She's . . . I don't know."

"She's very refined," Mary said, "quiet. A person just feels very respectful in her presence."

Oh, yeah? Terry thought dryly. The images in his mind that he'd had of Annabella when he'd heard her voice, seen her smile, were hardly respectful. Sensuous as hell, but not respectful.

"I think there's more to her than meets the eye," he said, continuing the steady motion of the swing.

"Such as?" Mike asked.

Terry shrugged. "I don't know. She . . . well, has a dimple in her right cheek that comes out of nowhere when she smiles. Her smile is a hundred-proof dazzler, too. And have you ever listened, really listened, to her voice? That is the sexiest—" He cleared his throat. "Forget it."

"Sexiest?" Mary prompted, leaning forward in her chair. "Miss Annabella has a sexy voice?"

"Yeah, she does," Terry said, shifting uncomfortably on the swing. "It's sort of husky, sensuous, and . . . could we change the subject? You're a mother, Mother. You're not supposed to take part in conversations like this."

"Pshaw," Mary said. "If I didn't know about sexy and sensuous, how would I have become a mother?"

Mike hooted with laughter.

"Oh, for Pete's sake," Terry said. "Change the subject."

Mary settled back in her chair. "Miss Annabella is in our Quilting Club. She never says much, but we're all years older than she is. She sews a lovely stitch. You know, I've always felt she could be a lot prettier if she just tried a tad more. I'm not one for getting all gussied up, you realize, but Miss Annabella needn't go around looking so drab. I've never seen her in anything but somber shades. She should wear bright, happy colors, maybe use a touch of makeup."

"She needs a man," Mike said.

Terry's head jerked around to look at his father. "What?"

"Yep," Mike said, puffing on his pipe. "Miss Annabella needs a good man in her life."

"That's a thought," Mary said, nodding.

"Well, it sure as hell shouldn't be Ralph Newberry," Terry said. "Excuse my language, Mother." He paused. "Dammit, Newberry is too old for her. Excuse me, Mother." He paused again. "Hell, Ralph is a dud. Excuse—"

"Terry," his mother said, "if you're going to swear,

then swear, for heaven's sake. Quit fumbling over your tongue apologizing every two seconds."

Terry narrowed his eyes. "You're not my mother. You're an impostor."

Mary laughed. "You're too big for me to wash out your mouth for swearing. So! You don't approve of Ralph Newberry for Miss Annabella?"

"No," Terry said gruffly. "He's dull as dishwater. She should have someone who will teach her about life, love, make her laugh, give her reason to smile that knockout smile of hers and . . ." His voice trailed off as he realized his parents were staring at him intently. "Actually, it's none of my business," he finished lamely.

Mary smiled. Mike puffed on his pipe.

"Hell," Terry muttered. He'd sure gone on and on like a motor-mouth about Annabella Abraham. But, dammit, she'd been buzzing around in his brain like a pesty bee all afternoon. He'd heard her voice over and over, seen her smile and the sparkle that came into her dark eyes. And with the mental images came the coil of heat low in his body, stirring his blood.

Dammit, Terry fumed on, what was it about her, the little sparrow, that kept nagging at him, pulling at his thoughts, and wreaking havoc with his libido? She wasn't his type. Lord, was she ever not his type. But there was just something intriguing about her, like . . . like a Christmas present waiting to be unwrapped to reveal the mystery and surprise within. Slowly unwrapped, gently, carefully, then . . .

"Well," Terry said, a trifle too loudly as he felt his

manhood surge with heat, "it sure is a nice night, isn't it?"

Mike chuckled. Terry slid him a dark look.

"Phone is ringing," Mary said, getting to her feet. "It's probably Esther Sue calling about the bake sale. Miss Annabella makes wonderful sugar tea-cookies and bakes the most delicious bread."

A silence fell on the porch with the sounds of summer in the distance: Crickets singing their special song, a hoot owl calling to the night, locusts humming in the grass. The swing creaked as Terry moved it slowly back and forth.

"You know," Mike said quietly, placing his pipe in the ashtray, "I meant what I said about Miss Annabella needing a man in her life."

Terry shrugged, but didn't comment.

"But forget Miss Annabella for a minute, Terry, and think about yourself. You need a woman, a wife and family. You were happy when you were married to Misty. You were meant to be a husband and father. There are very few men who do well living their lives without the gentle touch of women, their wives, by their sides. We need what they offer us. Oh, I don't mean just in bed, I'm talking about their wisdom, their way of seeing life. They're remarkable creatures, women. Lord knows I'd hate to be going through this life without your mother. You've been alone too long, Terry. You're not still mourning for Misty, are you?"

"No, Dad. I had a rough time after she died, even though I knew that I couldn't have prevented it, that I had done all I could. She was so healthy, so full of life, then suddenly she was so damned sick. It all happened so fast."

"Which was a blessing, in a way," Mike said.

"Yeah, I know." Terry stopped the swing and dropped his foot to the floor, leaning forward to rest his elbows on his knees and making a steeple of his fingers. "I never told anyone this before, Dad, but it was as though I lost Misty twice."

"What do you mean, Son?" Mike asked gently.

"I lost her in death, and I kept her memory close to me, made sure she was there in my mind wherever I went. Then . . ." Terry stopped speaking. Mike waited patiently. "Then, it was about two years after she'd died, and I started having trouble remembering what her smile looked like, how her laughter sounded. I couldn't remember what her favorite color was, or if it had been beans or peas that she refused to eat. Lord, I felt guilty as hell because I was losing her again, and I couldn't seem to stop it from taking place."

"Terry, that was time healing your pain, preparing you to move forward with a heart and soul ready to love once more. Are you afraid to love, Son? Afraid you might suffer such a loss again?"

"I really don't know. If that's true, it's buried so deep inside of me, I'm not aware that it's there. I got the promotion at St. John Enterprises several years ago, I'm in charge of the staff of pilots, I'm on first call for the St. John family, and I handle most overseas flights. I have just poured my energy into my work. There are plenty of women around if I want them, but my flying is my life."

"Is it enough?"

"I love to fly. There's no way to explain it to someone who hasn't felt the power of a plane move up to the heavens under the command of their own hands. It's incredible."

"I'm sure it is, but is it enough? Terry, I know you came home for this vacation because you were tired. But did it ever occur to you that you might also be lonely?"

Terry's head snapped up and he looked over at his father.

"Think about it, Son," Mike said. "Do that for your old Dad, will you? Just think about what I said."

Terry stared at him for a long moment, then nodded slowly. "Yeah, I'll think about it."

"Fair enough." Mike got to his feet. "Well, I'm turning in. Pulling tree stumps is hard work for tired bones. Good night, Terry."

"See ya, Dad."

"Mike?" Mary asked, reappearing at the screen door. "Are you heading to bed? Well, I'll go with you. Terry, will you tend to the locking up when you come in?"

"Sure thing. Good night, Mom."

"Good night, Son," Mary said. "Oh, my Michael, you look so weary. You'll be asleep before your head hits the pillow, and you'll snore like an old bear."

"I don't snore."

"You do, you know it, and it's music to my ears, my own private lullaby."

Terry smiled as his parents walked arm-in-arm away from the door. His folks were so special together, he mused. They were as much in love, if not more so, as when they were a young couple just starting out. They'd struggled through the lean years, raised three energetic kids, and now they had just each other again, their lives intertwined and connected with an indestructible bond of love. They were really something.

The kitchen light was turned off, blanketing the porch in darkness. The stars twinkled overhead, and the creatures of the night continued their serenade. Terry leaned back, resuming the gentle motion of the swing.

Lonely.

The word his father had spoken echoed in Terry's mind, taunting him, forcing him to look deep within himself for an answer to the question he'd never before asked of himself.

Was he lonely?

A sudden shift of clouds covered the moon and stars, extinguishing the silvery glow. Terry had the irrational thought that he'd been cut off from the world, flung out into a dark abyss, and wouldn't be allowed to return until he'd found the answer to his question.

He sifted his life in his mind's eye, his days, his nights, the women, the parties, the fancy, exciting foreign countries. But he saw himself on the edge of it all, looking on, watching, there but not really there.

And in the solitude of the darkness, sitting on the swing where he'd spent hours in his youth, Terry Russell knew he was a very lonely man.

Was Annabella Abraham lonely, too? he wondered suddenly.

He laced his hands behind his head and slouched low in the swing, staring up into the darkness.

If she was lonely, did she realize it? Or did she just go through life not questioning anything, the way he had done, not recognizing the signs of loneliness? Did she have anyone who cared enough, as his father cared for him, to force her to take a good, long look deep within herself?

A sudden breeze sprang up, gusting to a strong wind in places, and Terry's attention was drawn from his thoughts to the sky overhead. It was as though with a huff and a puff the clouds were being blown away to reveal once more the silvery glow of the moon and the multitude of brightly twinkling stars.

Terry glowered at the sky, actually feeling as though he'd been released from his prison of darkness because he'd done as instructed and found his inner answer.

He walked to the edge of the porch and braced his hands high on the wooden framework of the door, staring up into the sky.

He felt so powerfully drawn to the little sparrow by strange, invisible threads. He had a mission to accomplish: Either Annabella would show him the tricks of the trade of being content alone, or he'd pass the baton of caring begun by his father and gently show Annabella that there was more to life than what she had, that she needed to fill the void also. This was crazy. He didn't even know how to talk to the woman, let alone figure out what she was thinking and feeling.

Terry threw up his hands. He had to do it, he

knew. He'd either learn from Annabella and tuck the knowledge away, on the outside chance he'd never find the right woman to love. Or, *he'd* teach *her* that life had more to offer than what she was taking from it.

Annabella Abraham, Terry realized, was about to be tightly interwoven in his life until he figured all this out. He'd have to approach her with finesse. If he came on like gangbusters, he'd scare her to death. It would be slow and easy, watch and listen, gather facts, put the pieces of the puzzle together.

He'd figure out a plan whereby he could see her, spend some time with her. He'd be able to hear that incredible, blood-churning voice, see that light-up-her-face smile if he played his cards right. He'd admittedly been intrigued with what might be beneath the somber, drab surface of Miss Annabella and was now determined to find out for reasons far more complex than simple male curiosity.

Okay, Terry thought decisively, onward and upward, full steam ahead—remembering not to scare Annabella out of her sensible shoes. One of them was going to get some answers. If Annabella was perfectly content, he'd keep what he'd learned from her in reserve in case he, too, was to face the future alone. If Annabella saw the light, he'd have the satisfaction of knowing he'd executed a caring plan, just as his father had done for him.

"Excellent," Terry said to the stars. "I've got this all figured out."

The next morning Annabella woke at the usual

time, despite the fact that she didn't have to go to the library. She automatically started to toss aside the blankets, then suddenly sank back against the pillows and stared up at the ceiling.

Something, she realized, was nagging at her, disturbing her. Whatever could be wrong? She'd spent a quiet evening reading, then she'd gone to bed at ten o'clock as usual, then . . .

"Oh, merciful saints," she said aloud, her hands flying to her cheeks. She'd dreamed about Terry Russell! And she'd been trying to take off his clothes! "Oh, Annabella," she said, horrified.

Well, she decided in the next instant, it wasn't as shameful as it might have been. After all, in her dream she'd never managed to accomplish the feat of disrobing Mr. Russell.

There had been constant interruptions. A pile of library books had suddenly appeared between them, and she'd had to carefully stack them out of the way. As she'd reached again for the top button on Terry's shirt, Clara and Susie had come zooming in with their shopping carts, stopping to chatter with Terry. Annabella's next attempt had been aborted by Ralph Newberry's asking for a tissue to blow his nose. Then Esther Sue had popped up, demanding to know why Annabella was late with her bread and sugar tea-cookies for the bake sale.

Terry had shrugged apologetically, tapped his watch with his fingertip, and said he had to fly around the world a couple of times in the airplane she'd won. Fully clothed, without even one button undone on his shirt, he waved before disappearing into a heavy fog.

"My stars," Annabella said, shaking her head. How embarrassing to think she'd had such a wanton dream. But if it fell into the category of a nocturnal romantic fantasy, it was rather, well, disappointing. It seemed only fair that she could have gotten the man's shirt off—at least.

Oh-h-h, she moaned inwardly, listen to her. How shameful. She, who was about to get up and prepare to go to Sunday church services, was pouting over not having ripped Terry Russell's shirt from his body in her ever-so-risqué dream.

"Have a cup of tea, Annabella," she said, and hurriedly got out of bed.

Annabella showered and shampooed. After blow-drying her heavy brown hair and brushing it until it shone, she started to put it into the usual bun. She hesitated. Sitting on the stool in front of her vanity, she tilted her head from one side to the other and watched her hair swing with the motion.

On impulse she braided it into a single plait, then twisted it into a figure eight at the back of her head, instantly relieved not to feel the weight of the bun on her neck. She left the top and sides slightly fuller and decided she didn't look quite so much like a skinned chicken.

Her dress was a silky gray shirtwaist, her shoes simple, gray low-heeled pumps. After her cup of spiced-apple tea, a piece of toast, and a bruised peach, she picked up her purse and left the house. As she stepped off the porch, she stopped to look at the row of geraniums.

Ten minutes later Annabella Abraham started down the sidewalk with a red geranium pinned to her dress above her left breast. Why she had suddenly decided to wear the vibrant flower, she didn't know. Nor was she sure why she'd changed her hairdo. She shrugged and continued on her way, quickening her step so as not to be late for church.

Terry entered the church with his parents and told himself yet again that the bright smile on his mother's face would be worth suffering through one of Pastor Peterson's fire-and-brimstone sermons.

The church was crowded, and Terry looked above the heads of those in the aisle for a place for them to sit. And then he saw her. Annabella. She was moving into the fifth pew.

"Come on," Terry said, taking his mother's elbow. "There's room closer up."

"There's room right here," Mary said, indicating the pew next to them.

"I don't want to miss a word of the great sermon we're going to hear," Terry said.

"We are?" Mike said. "Is there a visiting pastor today?"

"Mike, hush," Mary said. She gasped, as Terry nearly lifted her off of her feet and hauled her forward.

Mike frowned, glanced in the direction that Terry was dragging Mary, then smiled. He followed contentedly behind the pair.

Terry moved into the fifth pew, sat down, then patted his mother's knee as soon as she sat down next to him. Terry slowly turned his head.

"Why, Miss Annabella," he said, smiling brightly, "fancy meeting you here. Good morning." She looked

different somehow, he mused. Softer, more feminine . . . or something. Her hair. It wasn't pulled so
tightly back, nor was it on her neck. She had a
lovely throat: long, the color of ivory, skin like satin.
Drab gray dress, but the red flower was a really nice
touch. Really nice. Why was she staring at the top
button of his shirt instead of meeting his gaze? "Is
my shirt unbuttoned?"

Annabella's gaze flew up to meet his. "No," she
said, hearing the squeak in her voice. "That button
is not undone. It definitely is not."

Her cheeks were hot, she thought. She could feel
them burning. Oh, why had Terry sat next to her?
He looked wonderful in black slacks and a yellow
shirt. The sight of that buttoned shirt had brought
back every detail of her embarrassing dream. And
his lips. Mercy, she'd sat in her rocker and fantasized about those lips kissing hers. She wanted to
die, just slide off the pew and disappear.

"Are you all right, Miss Annabella?" Terry asked.
"You were flushed, but now you're pale."

"I'm fine, just fine."

"That's good," he said. Women with voices like
hers should not speak aloud in church, he decided.
Unholy things were happening to his libido.

The organ music began, and Terry glanced at the
numbers posted on the board on a front pillar as he
reached for a hymnal. Actually, he grabbed three
hymnals, quickly handing one to his father, another
to his mother.

"We'll share," he said to Annabella, then smiled
his best hundred-watt smile.

Everyone got to his feet and Terry flipped quickly through the pages.

"Great," he said, extending half of the book to Annabella. "My favorite hymn, 'Onward, Christian Soldiers.' "

The organ stopped for a moment, then started again. Annabella jerked in surprise as Terry began to belt out "Onward, Christian Soldiers" in the loudest, most off-key voice she had ever heard. She gripped her half of the hymnal and stared up at him with wide eyes. He was looking straight ahead, singing his heart out, giving it his awful all.

And Annabella Abraham, in the middle of the fifth pew of the crowded church, laughed.

Why she was laughing, she had no idea, except that it suddenly seemed hysterically funny. There he was, great big, gorgeous Terry Russell, jet-setter, big-city, world-flying pilot. Terry Russell, singing in a voice that would make babies cry. Terry Russell, who caused wives and mothers and quiet librarians to fantasize about wanton things because he was just so beautiful, presently sounded like a wounded bull in the little church in Harmony, Oklahoma.

And to Annabella, that was funny.

Terry peered at her out of the corner of his eye, then did a quick double take as he saw her clamp her hand over her mouth. Her eyes were sparkling like diamonds and her shoulders were shaking. She met his gaze, then rolled her eyes to the heavens as she tried to control her merriment, her hand still over her mouth.

Terry leaned down and whispered in her ear. "What is your problem?"

She shook her head vigorously.

He frowned. "My singing," he whispered. "That's it, isn't it? You don't like my singing. Annabella Abraham, are you laughing at *me*?"

She bobbed her head up and down.

Terry hooted with laughter, which earned him a sharp elbow in the ribs from his mother.

"Mother," he said, in a loud whisper, "Miss Annabella is laughing at my singing."

"She has good taste," Mike said calmly.

Mary peered past Terry to speak to Annabella. "I know it's dreadful, dear, but he isn't home often enough to mention it. We just suffer through."

"Well, thanks," Terry said indignantly. "I've been thoroughly insulted."

"A-men," the congregation sang.

Everyone sat down. Terry looked straight ahead. Annabella removed her hand from her mouth, drew a steadying breath, then folded her hands primly in her lap.

As Pastor Peterson welcomed everyone and made the weekly announcements, including one regarding the upcoming bake sale, Terry turned his head slightly to look at Annabella. At the exact same instant she peered cautiously at him.

And they smiled at each other.

It was a quiet moment, a sharing moment, a we-were-naughty-but-wasn't-it-fun? moment. It was Terry looking at Annabella, and she at him, and time stopped. Their smiles faded, but still they looked at each other, forgetting where they were and what they were supposed to be doing.

Terry's heart thundered in his chest.

A flutter danced along Annabella's spine.

It wasn't until the congregation rose that the two of them blinked and looked around, getting up quickly.

She was a spell-weaver, Terry thought, this delightful Annabella. He'd heard her rich, melodic laughter. Her eyes had been sensational, dancing with merriment. And when he'd looked at her again, he'd been pinned in place, unable to move. Oh, there was most definitely more to Annabella Abraham than met the eye.

She'd laughed in church, Annabella thought incredulously. She couldn't believe this. And then, when Terry had looked at her . . . what had happened? She'd felt so strange, so warm and cold at the same time. Oh, heavens above, what was this man doing to her?

"Let us pray," Pastor Peterson said.

Good idea, Annabella thought, rather hysterically. She needed all the help she could get in figuring out why her world had suddenly become topsy-turvy since Terry Russell had arrived.

Three

Annabella hardly remembered the remainder of the Sunday services. It was as though an invisible hand had flicked a switch and turned all her senses on red alert.

She could feel the heat from Terry's leg when it brushed against hers, heat that inched its way up, through, and around her body. She caught whiffs of his woodsy after-shave and an aroma she thought was perhaps a combination of soap and just plain male essence. She saw the power of Terry's body, the muscles moving beneath his slacks, in his arms, his shoulders, and his back. She heard the rich timbre of his speaking voice, and his god-awful singing was etched indelibly in her mind.

And she was aware, as never before, of herself. Where Terry was hard, taut, rugged, she was soft, gently curved, smaller, more delicately built. Her breasts grew heavy with the now familiar aching sensation, which caused her eyes to stray to Terry's hands. Hands she just somehow knew would feel like heaven itself when they touched her, would soothe the strange, sweet pain in her breasts. She could hear the wild thudding of her own heart echoing in her ears and could feel a warm flush on her cheeks. Only one of her senses was missing, Annabella thought dreamily. Taste. And that one . . . oh, yes . . . that one would come in the form of the taste of Terry's kiss when he claimed her lips with his.

"Well, let's do it," Terry said. He slapped his hands onto his thighs and got to his feet.

Annabella rose slowly and blinked; then the two separate parts of her came back together with a thud. Terry's words registered in her brain, and she had the panicky thought that she'd spoken aloud of how her sense of taste was to be satisfied.

She looked up at him with wide eyes. "Pardon me?" she asked, her voice unsteady.

"It's over. Let's get out of here," Terry said. "It's warm, and I could use some fresh air." And some space between him and Annabella Abraham, he thought grimly. She'd driven him crazy! His leg had kept bumping her very soft leg, she smelled like flowers, and he'd suddenly become very aware that she had full breasts, very full breasts, pushing against the material of her dress. Warm was not an adequate word. Hot was closer to the mark. And in church, for crying out loud. Lightning was probably going to strike him dead on the spot.

"Dad, can't you move out of the pew more quickly?" Terry asked.

"In a minute," Mike said, then continued to speak to Mary. Mary nodded. Mike went into the aisle.

Pastor Peterson greeted people at the door as they left, and Terry complimented him on the sermon, which he hadn't heard a word of. Out on the sidewalk friends and neighbors spoke to the Russells, many telling Terry how good it was to see him home.

Annabella tried to edge her way through the gathering. She wanted to go home, lock her door, and never come out again. Her behavior that morning had been absolutely terrible, and she was totally mortified.

"Miss Annabella," Mary said, "would you do us the honor of joining us for lunch? We have our big meal at noon on Sundays, and it's in my slow-cooker just waiting to be put on the table. We'd love to have you."

"Me?" Annabella said.

"It would be our pleasure, Miss Annabella," Mike said. "Right, Terry?"

"Huh? Oh, yeah, right. You bet," Terry said, nodding. Oh, man, not today. Tomorrow maybe, but not today!

"Oh, well, thank you very much," Annabella said, "but I really don't . . ."

"Shall we?" Terry said. What the hell, he thought. Go with the flow. He lifted Annabella's hand and tucked it in the crook of his arm. "My Mom creates wonders in her slow-cooker. You can tell us everything we ever wanted to know about libraries, books, all that. Mom, Dad, you take the car. Miss Annabella and I will walk. My muscles are tight from being crammed into the pew. You can check your slow-cooker, Mom, to make sure it's cooking slow . . . or whatever. Okay? See you at the house."

"But . . ." Mary said.

"Fine plan," Mike said, taking Mary's arm. "Come along, dear."

"Why is everyone dragging me around today?" Mary muttered as she went with Mike.

"You don't mind walking, do you?" Terry asked Annabella. "Did you bring your car?"

"No, I walked, but . . ."

"Good, let's go," Terry said, starting down the sidewalk.

"Terry Russell, you call me, you hear?" a female voice yelled. "We've got some unfinished business, darlin'."

Terry lifted a hand, but didn't look back to see whom he was acknowledging.

Annabella peered over her shoulder. "Casey Mae Templeton," she whispered. "Casey Mae Templeton?"

"Old news," Terry said cheerfully. "Haven't seen her in years."

"She's been married three times."

"Is that a fact? Guess she's going to practice until she gets it right." They crossed the street and started down the next block, Annabella's hand still in the crook of Terry's arm. "So, tell me, Miss Annabella, do you plan to marry?" *Slick, Russell*, he told himself. *Very nice. Get to the personal stuff.* He had to gather his data, find out if Annabella Abraham was lonely. "Well?"

"No, I don't think so."

"Why not?"

"Well, because . . ." Her voice trailed off. What was

she supposed to say? she wondered. She couldn't tell Terry that men never noticed her and that she wouldn't know what to do or say if they did. She couldn't tell him that she'd long ago given up her hopes and dreams of being a wife and mother, and had accepted herself and her life as it was. "Just—" she shrugged, "because."

So much for that, Terry thought. She really hadn't answered the question. He'd press a little bit more.

"I hear that Ralph Newberry is quite taken with you, Miss Annabella," he said, looking down at her. He watched her face carefully.

"Oh, dear," she said, wrinkling her nose, "I was afraid of that. He's such a . . . I don't mean to be unkind . . . but he's such a twit."

An unexpected rush of relief swept through Terry, and a wide smile broke across his face.

"Does he still have those allergies?" he asked.

"Goodness, yes. He just blows his nose, and blows his nose, and—mercy, I don't usually talk about people this way. I'm not being very nice." She paused. "Do you plan to remarry?"

"I most definitely hope so."

Annabella's eyes flew up to look at him. "You do? But Susie and Clara said—never mind. I'm not one to gossip. This isn't like me at all." She fiddled with her hair with her free hand. "But then I haven't been behaving true to form ever since . . . it must be the heat."

"Or something. Is your hair long?"

"My hair?" she said, looking up at him again. "Yes, it's long, I guess. It comes to the middle of my back. It's awfully heavy. Maybe I should cut it."

"No!" Terry said sharply. Annabella jerked in surprise. "That is, I'm sure it's lovely. You should wear it loose and free sometimes."

"Oh, I don't think so," Annabella said, smiling. "That's hardly the proper image for a librarian."

"But you're not always a librarian," Terry said, "just like I'm not always a pilot. You're also a woman, and I'm a man."

If he knew how very conscious she was of that, Annabella thought dryly, she'd slip through a crack in the sidewalk.

"Well, yes, of course, I realize that," she said.

Terry stopped so suddenly that Annabella nearly tripped. She looked at him questioningly.

"Do you?" he asked, his voice low as he gazed directly into her eyes.

"Do I what?" There was a thread of breathlessness in her voice. "I forgot the question."

"Do you realize that you're a woman and I'm a man?" he asked. He wanted to kiss her, he thought. Right in the shade of the big old oak tree they were standing under. He wanted, he needed, to kiss Annabella Abraham.

"Yes," she said softly. "I'm very much aware of that fact, Terry."

He lifted his hands to cradle her face. "Ma'am." He lowered his head toward hers. "I'm extremely pleased to hear you say so."

"Oh, but I . . ."

"Extremely pleased," he said before covering her lips with his.

Taste, Annabella thought, her lashes drifting down.

This was the delicious taste of Terry Russell. His lips were so soft, so warm, so . . .

"Open your mouth for me, Annabella," he murmured.

Her eyes popped back open and her lips parted in shock at his request.

"Good girl," he said. He took possession of her mouth once again, his tongue slipping into the sweet darkness.

Annabella went ramrod stiff, her eyes as wide as saucers. But then . . . then something changed. Her eyes drifted closed again as a marvelous warmth consumed her and began to pulse deep within her in a rhythm that matched the stroking of Terry's tongue over and around hers.

Never, she thought, had she been kissed like this. Never. And never before had she felt so feminine and special, and even pretty. And never, never before had she experienced such a wondrous yearning . . . desire. She was, indeed, a woman, and Terry Russell was every inch a man.

Oh-h-h, Lord, Terry thought, what a kiss. He had to stop. He would stop. In a minute. Or an hour. Annabella tasted so good, and her lips were custom-made just for him. There was passion hiding beneath the surface of the little sparrow, and he wanted more of it, and more, much more, of Annabella Abraham.

Terry slowly, reluctantly, lifted his head, his hands still framing her face. "Oh, Annabella," he said, his voice slightly raspy, "you kiss like a dream."

She opened her eyes. "I do?" She blinked. "No, I

don't. *You* kissed *me*. I've never kissed anyone the way . . . that is . . ."

"Did you hate it?" he asked, smiling at her.

"No, no, it was . . . lovely. Thank you."

"Don't thank me as though I gave you something. We shared that kiss equally. You did kiss me, Annabella, whether or not you realize it or want to admit it. And it was, I must say, a helluva kiss."

"Oh," she said, then smiled. "Oh, well, fancy that."

Terry chuckled, dropped his hands from her face, and tucked her hand back in the crook of his arm. They started off again. Annabella glanced quickly around.

"What's wrong?"

"I'm not in the habit of kissing men in the middle of the sidewalk in broad daylight. I just hope no one saw us."

"Don't worry about it." He paused. "Are you in the habit of kissing men at all?"

Annabella sighed. "No, not much. I guess you could tell. I mean, you're a very experienced man."

"I am?" He grinned down at her.

"You know you are. And I'm not . . . that is to say . . . oh, mercy, I can't believe I kissed you in the middle of the sidewalk in broad daylight. What on earth is happening to me?"

"There's nothing wrong with a kiss, Annabella," Terry said. "You're being too hard on yourself. We enjoyed that kiss, both of us." No joke. "In fact, I imagine I'll kiss you again at the first opportunity." Now. Right now. Dammit, lighten up, he told himself sternly. "Calm down, okay?"

"But you see, it's more than just the kiss. I had a

dream about—saints above, Annabella, shut up," she said, shaking her head.

Terry slid his arm around her shoulders and tucked her close to his side as they continued to walk. Annabella was totally off balance, he realized. She hadn't even noticed he'd pulled her close to him. She was frowning, looking upset. Poor little sparrow. He had to show her, convince her, make her understand, that she'd done nothing wrong. What was happening to her? Could she be learning that a very passionate woman was slumbering within her? Perhaps. And, if so, she was probably scared to death.

Well, Terry rambled on to himself, there was nothing for Annabella to be frightened of. He was there, was going to take care of her as she took her first steps into the world of womanliness. Annabella deserved to know who she really was, what was waiting for her as she left her nest. He was going to help her like . . . a friend? A big brother? Forget it. Neither of those labels fit the way he was feeling at the moment.

This was all part of his research, he told himself, his mission, his purpose. Until Annabella discovered her full potential, she couldn't begin to know if she was really happy or if she was lonely. And he couldn't learn from her how to be happy alone unless she truly wished to live her life that way. Before he went back to New York, he would have his answers and Annabella would have hers. When he left her, they'd both be squared away.

Terry quickly looked down at Annabella, who was still frowning. Left her? his mind echoed. Well, of course. He was only home on vacation, his life was no longer in Harmony, Oklahoma.

But the thought of leaving her was disturbing. That made sense. Sure it did. He was feeling very protective of Annabella Abraham at the moment because he'd kissed her on the sidewalk in broad daylight, had upset her, and had every intention of going further. He owed it to Annabella to do this for her, just as his father had nudged him to take a hard look at himself. Annabella would thank him for this someday. In the meantime he was sticking to her like glue so she wouldn't be frightened.

Annabella sighed. It was a sad sigh, a confused, weary-sounding sigh, and Terry's hold on her tightened.

"Annabella," he said gently, "trust me, all right? You haven't done anything wrong, not one damned thing."

"I even laughed in church," she said miserably.

Terry chuckled. "With just cause, according to the vote taken. Here's the house. Let's go in and see what my mom has slow-cooked in the slow-cooker."

Annabella managed a small smile. "You must think I'm acting like a ridiculous child."

"No, I think you're behaving like a woman who is just now discovering exactly how much of a woman she is."

"A little late, wouldn't you say?"

"No way. There's no official timetable for any of this. Every person operates at his or her own speed."

"I bet you were very speedy, very early."

Terry laughed, then dropped his arm from her shoulders and motioned toward the house. Annabella hesitated, then lifted her chin and marched up the front walk. Terry's gaze skimmed over her, seeing her tiny waist, the gentle slope of her hips beneath the clinging material of her dress, her shapely calves.

"Definitely a woman," he muttered, then followed her into the house.

To her own amazement Annabella relaxed and thoroughly enjoyed lunch. The meal of chicken, noodles, and fresh vegetables was delicious. For dessert Mary Russell had made a cherry pie, which was heaped with vanilla ice cream. The conversation was fast and lively, the Russells all possessing a quick sense of humor and the ability to laugh at themselves.

The Russell home wasn't terribly large and had a comfortable, lived-in aura about it that seemed to wrap itself around Annabella in a welcoming cloak. It was a family house full of warmth and caring. Annabella saw the gentle glances that passed between Mary and Mike, and the glow of pride in their eyes when they looked at Terry.

There was deep love within these walls, Annabella mused; even more special, the Russells did not seem to take that love for granted. She sensed that they cherished what they had together.

Terry told the story of when he'd climbed on the roof to spy on one of his sisters, who was sitting on the screened porch with her beau. His other rotten sister, he said, had taken the ladder away, and Terry was stuck up there for hours until his parents arrived home to rescue him.

Annabella had laughed in delight, then blushed

crimson when she'd met Terry's gaze and found him smiling warmly at her.

"Did you grow up in Tulsa, Miss Annabella?" Mary asked as they finished their pie.

"Yes, I went to a Catholic boarding school. My father died when I was four, and my mother was frail. She couldn't cope with raising a child alone. As soon as I was old enough I went to the school to be raised by the nuns. My mother died when I was twelve."

"Bessie Montgomery was your aunt?" Mike said.

"Yes, but I didn't know she existed until the lawyer contacted me about the funeral and the house she'd left me. Apparently, Aunt Bessie and my mother had a falling-out many years ago. I was amazed to discover I had an aunt. All those years at the school I thought . . . well, that I was totally alone."

And lonely, Terry thought. He'd make book on it. Annabella had been a very lonely little girl. Question was, had she grown up to be a lonely woman?

"What a shame that Bessie didn't contact you earlier," Mary said, shaking her head.

"Well," Annabella said, "she had her reasons, I guess. It was awfully good of her to leave me the house on Peach Street. It's very nice, and I like Harmony much more than I did Tulsa."

"Most of the young people are eager to leave here," Mike said.

"I'm very content," Annabella said. Wasn't she? Of course she was. She had everything she needed right there in Harmony. Just because she'd been acting like a silly goose since Terry arrived didn't mean she wasn't perfectly satisfied with the overall pattern of her life.

Annabella was surprised when both Terry and Mike helped clear the table and put the leftovers away. Annabella rinsed the dishes, Mary put them in the dishwasher, and all evidence of the delicious meal was whisked out of sight. It was a joint effort, a family effort, and Annabella realized she was having a lovely time.

"Thank you so much for inviting me," she said at last.

"It was our pleasure, dear," Mary said. "Don't rush off. We can all relax on the screened porch. That's where we spend lazy Sunday afternoons."

"If I can borrow the car, Dad, I thought Annabella and I might drive out to the new man-made lake. I haven't seen it yet," Terry said.

" 'If I can borrow the car, Dad,' " Mike said, with a chuckle. He handed Terry the keys. "Brings back a memory or two."

"Indeed it does," Mary said. "Well, go along then, and have a good time."

"Have you seen the lake, Annabella?" Terry asked.

"No, but—"

"Then we'll see it together. Do they have changing rooms out there, Dad? Or should we wear our bathing suits under our clothes?"

"The changing rooms aren't up yet, according to an article in the paper," Mike said. "Mary, do we have any beach towels?"

"In the linen closet," Mary said. "I'll get them. It's a perfect day for a swim."

"Oh, but—" Annabella started again.

"I'll go change," Terry said. "I'll be right back, Annabella, then we'll stop by your house so you can get into your suit."

"But, I—"

"Can you swim, Miss Annabella?" Mike asked pleasantly as Terry and his mother left the room.

"No, I can't. I never go in past my knees. Does Terry always zoom around like this? I mean, he's so energetic."

Mike laughed. "He's a doer, all right. Always on the go. He wears himself to a frazzle sometimes. That's why he's home on vacation now. He's all worn out."

"If that's worn out, I'd hate to see him well rested," Annabella said.

Mike laughed in delight. Mary reappeared with two large striped towels. Terry came back. Annabella looked him over, then made herself close her mouth, which had dropped open.

Terry was wearing faded cutoff jeans with frayed edges and a green T-shirt that said PILOTS DO IT IN THE CLOUDS. The shirt stretched tightly across his broad shoulders and muscled chest, and his legs were tanned and beautifully proportioned, boasting a smattering of white-blond hair. He was, Annabella thought wistfully, magnificent.

"That shirt is a disgrace," Mary said.

Terry peered down at the slogan. "Catchy, huh? I think it's great. Ready to go, Annabella?"

"Well, I—" she threw up her hands—"I guess so, but it's only fair to tell you that I don't know how to swim." "Annabella," she mused. He didn't call her "Miss Annabella," he said "Annabella," and it sounded so pretty when spoken in that rich, deep voice of his. Enough. She was getting giddy again.

"You can splash around and cool off," Terry said.

"Best wait awhile before you go in the water," Mary said. "You just ate."

"I'm watching the time," Terry said. "Annabella still has to change, then we have to drive out there. It ought to work out just right. See you later."

"Yep," Mike said, lighting his pipe. "Enjoy yourselves."

"Thank you again for lunch," Annabella said. "I really did have a lovely—oh!" she gasped, as Terry grabbed her hand and started toward the door.

"Ignore him when he does that, dear," Mary said. "It's really so rude."

Mike just puffed contently on his pipe, a very pleased smile on his face.

It seemed to Annabella that before she'd had time to take a steadying breath, she was standing in her bedroom wondering where on earth she'd put her bathing suit, which she hadn't used in years. And wondering how it had happened that she was about to go swimming with Terry Russell at the new man-made lake. And wondering if this was how it felt when a person lost her mind.

Because, she decided, staring into space, she had a feeling she was rapidly approaching borderline cuckoo. The things she had done, the bizarre thoughts she'd entertained, the vivid dream she'd experienced, all of which centered on Terry, were shifting in her brain. Once harshly embarrassing, they were now softened by a lovely, rosy glow of delicious memories. Shameful was changing into blissful. Mortifying into marvelous. Wanton into wonderful.

"Annabella," she ordered herself, "find your bathing suit."

She pulled a box from her closet and began digging through it. And that was another thing. She was about to go parading around half-naked—because when one wore a bathing suit, one really was quite exposed—in front of Terry. A bathing suit would "tell it like it was," and her figure had no business telling anybody anything. Terry was in for a very unpleasant shock, and she'd be back to mortified.

But then came the nutty part, she thought, yanking the suit from the box. She wanted to go to the lake with Terry. She really did want to go. It sounded like fun, and it had been ever so long since she'd had any fun. And she wanted to be with Terry. And she definitely wanted to see *him* parading around half-naked in *his* bathing suit.

As Annabella removed her dress she absently wondered if anyone in Harmony would remember her after they came and carted her off to a padded cell.

Terry wandered around the small living room, deciding it was cozy and nice, very charming. He smiled as he saw the tiny bouquet of silk violets in a vase and the framed picture of violets on the wall.

It was too bad, he mused, that Annabella hadn't won the dishes with the violets on the border instead of the Cessna. No, then he probably wouldn't have met her. And he was very glad he'd met Annabella

Abraham. She was unique, rare, and very special. She was vulnerable and innocent and naive. She needed protecting from the kind of man who would take advantage of her lack of worldliness and experience. She needed protecting from . . . him? Well, hell, no. He hadn't done anything wrong. The kiss hadn't been disgraceful, it had been fantastic.

Terry fiddled with a throw pillow on the end of the sofa as he continued his inner dialogue. The kiss had proved a point and provided important information for his data gathering. Annabella Abraham was a very passionate woman. He was opening new doors for her, showing her other options available to her. Whether or not she chose to explore them was up to her.

Yes, he decided, his program was going well. He'd lead Annabella forward, slowly and carefully, then wait and watch to see what road she took. If she hightailed it back to the life she'd always had, he'd observe her further to see how she obtained contentment while alone. If she went the other way, emerged as the woman she was beneath the outer trimmings of the little brown sparrow, he'd pat himself on the back for a job well done.

But who, he wondered, what man would reap the rewards of Annabella, the woman, in full bloom if she went in that direction? How would she know, in her innocence, who was conning her and who was sincere? What if some joker broke her heart? Lord, it would be all his fault. He was the one awakening her femininity, her womanliness. He had a responsibility here.

Damn, he thought, how would he teach her how to

recognize a hustle and a bunch of bull? There were some real creeps out there who would see Annabella as easy pickings. He'd better think this through, give it very careful consideration in case Annabella decided to go for it and become the woman he knew she could be.

"Heavy, heavy, heavy," Terry said, shaking his head.

He picked up the newspaper from the coffee table and sank into the sofa, deciding he was going to wear out his brain if he didn't give it a rest.

Ten minutes later Annabella opened her bedroom door and stepped into the living room. Terry got slowly to his feet, his eyes sliding over her from top to bottom, then retracing their path.

Annabella was wearing a huge straw hat with a wide brim that flopped over in the front nearly to her nose. From neck to ankles she was covered in a tentlike creation of heavy dark purple material that hung in overlapping folds. On her arm she carried a faded blue canvas tote bag, and her feet were encased in sturdy brown loafers.

"Well . . . ," Terry started, then cleared his throat. "Do you think you'll be warm enough?" He paused. "Annabella, aren't you a little overdressed? It's very hot today."

"Oh, not at all," she said, tipping the brim of the hat up to look at him. "This is a cover-up. That's an official term for something one wears over one's bathing suit."

"Oh, I see," Terry said slowly. "You have your suit on under that . . . thing?"

"Yes, I do," she said, smiling pleasantly.

"Well, we'd better hurry on out to the lake before you fall over from heat stroke."

"I'm ready when you are."

Terry's gaze slid over her again, and he shook his head slightly as though not quite believing what he was seeing.

"Let's go," he said gruffly, starting toward the door. He stopped and waited for her. "By the way, I just saw in the newspaper that there's a rodeo today over in Castle Cove. That's a very popular event. We just might have the lake to ourselves. Our own private lake, Annabella. Cozy, huh?"

Annabella's pleasant smile faded as she preceded Terry out the door. A cluster of butterflies seemed to take up residency in her stomach as she absorbed the implication of Terry's announcement.

Cozy? she repeated in her mind. Scary was a better word. Private lake? Oodles of people were supposed to be at a lake on a hot day. Lots of folks: young, old, babies, teenagers, grandmas and grandpas, the whole gang. What kind of idiots went to a rodeo in Castle Cove when they could be at the new man-made lake in Harmony?

Oh, dear. Oh, dear. Oh, dear.

Four

The man-made lake was exactly twenty and four-tenths miles from the city limits of Harmony. It was also twenty and four-tenths miles from the city limits of Castle Cove.

The equal distance between the two towns was due to the fact that both towns had funded the project. It had taken nearly three years to raise the money, then another year to construct the lake and have the landscaping done. Except for the changing rooms all was ready, at exactly twenty and four-tenths miles between the two towns.

"I understand they haven't named the lake yet," Terry said to Annabella as they drove out of town.

"No," she said, "they can't agree on a name. The city councils of Harmony and Castle Cove are trying to come up with a fair way to do it."

Terry chuckled. "They could always have a drawing. You know, people could fill out tickets with their ideas for the name of the lake and put them in a big barrel."

Annabella flipped up the floppy edge of her hat so that she could give Terry a thorough glare. "Please don't even mention such a thing to me," she said. "The last time I got involved in that type of nonsense, I ended up owning an airplane." And ended up meeting Terry Russell, who was turning her life upside down.

"I'm going to start calling around about the plane tomorrow," he said. "I'll keep you posted. There's the lake up ahead. Hey, look at all that grass and the trees. It's an oasis."

"It is lovely, isn't it?" Annabella said, peering beneath the brim of her hat. "I've only seen pictures of it in the newspaper. The water is so blue, and . . . look, they even have a sandy beach surrounding it. The article in the paper said that the lake is nearly a mile wide. It's just so pretty."

Terry glanced quickly over at Annabella, a smile instantly on his face as he saw the sparkle in her eyes, the bright smile lighting up her features and showing off to perfection the dimple in her cheek. Even when she was animated, her voice, which caused his blood to quicken, was still sensuous, still sultry.

Right now, Terry decided, Annabella was a combination of a very alluring woman and an eager little girl about to see and experience something new and exciting for the first time. Lord, she was incredible, this Annabella Abraham. Even in her dreadful cover-up and the hat, which was the funniest, most ridiculous thing he'd ever seen, she was pulling at his senses.

Terry shook his head slightly in wonder, then drove slowly around to the opposite side of the lake.

"It wasn't crowded on that other side," Annabella said, looking over at him.

"This side looks nicer, has more grass, trees. There, see? There's some nice grass under that group of trees. We can be in the shade when we're not in the water. It's very private and . . . cozy."

"Oh," she said, in a small voice.

A short time later Terry had carried a blanket and the two beach towels to the secluded spot beneath the trees. He spread out the blanket, dropped the towels on top of it, and looked at Annabella.

"Ready to get your feet wet?" he asked.

"My feet?" she said, looking down at her loafers. "Oh, well, yes, I guess I could do that, couldn't I?" She stepped out of her shoes. "There, I'm ready."

"Annabella," Terry said gently, "you simply can't go out there in the direct hot sun in that heavy cover-up gizmo. You'll get overheated for sure." He reached for the bottom of his T-shirt. "Let's strip down to our bathing suits, okay?"

"Strip—" Annabella swallowed, "down?"

"Figure of speech," he said, then pulled his T-shirt up and away, dropping it onto the blanket.

That chest, Annabella thought wildly. What a chest. What a beautiful, tanned, muscled chest, covered in blond curls. The strip of hair narrowed and disappeared below the waistband of his cutoffs. Terry was reaching for the snap on his jeans! Oh, heavenly days, the zipper. He was inching it down, down some more, and . . .

Annabella peered beneath the brim of her hat, her

eyes riveted on Terry. There they go, she thought giddily. The cutoffs were—plop—right on the ground. The man had just disrobed, taken off his clothes! Those legs. Such nicely muscled thighs, and that dab of light hair, and . . . my, my, a white bathing suit. Snug, formfitting over narrow hips, and out-lining . . . she wanted to go home. She couldn't handle this. She was supposed to say something, she was sure of it, but what?

"Annabella?" Terry said.

She shifted her gaze upward, slowly, deciding she might as well enjoy the magnificent masculine view once more as long as her eyes were in the vicinity anyway. She looked at his face . . . finally.

"Well?" he said.

See, Annabella? she told herself. She was sup-posed to say something. Okay, she'd say, "I think you have a beautiful body, Terry." There. That should do it.

Terry choked, then whopped himself on the chest to get his breath. "What?" he croaked.

"You do," she said, smiling brightly. "Your body is splendid. Yes, you have a splendid body. That's my analysis, and the answer to your 'Well?' " She nod-ded in satisfaction.

"Oh, I see," he said. "Thank you for the nice com-pliment, but my 'Well?' was to ask why you hadn't taken off your cover-up."

"It was? Oh. I thought I was supposed to say . . . oh. My cover-up."

"Do you need some help with it?"

"No!" she said quickly. "No, I can do it. Thank you for offering, but I'm quite capable of disengaging myself from my cover-up."

Terry smiled. "Okay. Then go ahead and disengage before you pass out from the heat."

"Yes, I certainly will," she said. She didn't move.

Terry reached over and plucked the hat from her head. "There. Now, you do the rest."

"Absolutely," Annabella said, nodding. She undid the three buttons at the top of the cover-up, crossed her arms to grab handfuls of material, and began to inch the bulky outfit upward. "Here I go."

It was, without a doubt, Terry quickly determined, one of the most seductive performances he'd ever seen. He knew that Annabella's slow removal of the cover-up was due to her embarrassment. His brain knew that, but his body definitely didn't.

Long, long slender legs inched their way into Terry's view. Shapely legs. Legs that looked satiny were calling to him to slide his hands over the skin where the purple material had been. Annabella's bathing suit was blue, robin's-egg blue. It was one-piece, and it lovingly hugged the gentle slope of her hips and the flat plane of her stomach.

The cover-up went higher. Heat thudded low and heavy in Terry's body. He forgot to breathe, then remembered when his chest started to hurt. Higher. Then up and off and . . .

Holy smoke, Terry's mind thundered. He was dying.

Annabella's suit had a V in front that dipped to the middle of her breasts, exposing just a glimpse of the edge of their fullness. She was stunning! She had a knockout figure. She was sensational. The little sparrow was all woman.

He cleared his throat roughly. "Well. Yes, well, I must say, Annabella, that you . . . that your bathing suit . . . what I mean is . . . ah, hell, Annabella, you look fantastic."

Annabella blinked. "I look . . . what?"

Terry's heated gaze skimmed over her from head to toe, then he met her gaze.

"You don't know, do you?" he said. "You have no idea how attractive, how appealing, how womanly, you look standing there."

"I have skinny legs, and my breasts are too big, and—oh, heavens, I didn't mean to mention my breasts. That's not ladylike."

Terry stepped closer and cupped her throat lightly with his hands, tracing the line of her jaw with his thumbs.

"You have beautiful legs," he said, his voice slightly gritty. "Long, long, satiny legs." He lowered his head toward hers. "And your breasts are wonderful." He brushed his lips over hers. "They make me ache to touch them, feel their weight in my hands, taste them as I take each nipple slowly, so slowly, deep into my mouth."

"Dear heaven," Annabella whispered, as her knees began to tremble.

"I'm going to kiss you now, Annabella," Terry said, close to her lips. "You don't mind, do you?"

"No, no, not at all. That sounds quite lovely."

"Good. I'll try for lovely, really give it my best shot."

Terry's mouth melted over hers, his tongue slipping inside to meet hers in the sweet darkness.

Oh . . . how . . . lovely, Annabella thought dreamily.

Terry dropped his hands from her throat to her back as Annabella lifted her arms to circle his neck. He pulled her up against him, crushing her full breasts to his chest. He spread his legs slightly to fit her to the cradle of his hips, and the kiss intensified.

My goodness, Annabella thought, her lashes fanning her cheeks. She felt so strange and there was such heat swirling inside of her. Her breasts were aching again, were pressed to the hard wall of Terry's chest. Breasts he'd said were wonderful. Breasts he wanted to touch with his hands and . . . and with his mouth. Yes, she wanted to experience that. Shame on her, but she did!

Terry groaned as his hands moved to the delectable curve of Annabella's buttocks, moving her closer yet against his heated, straining manhood.

Lord, he thought foggily, she fit next to him so perfectly. She felt so damn good and tasted so damn good. And he wanted her. He would show her, teach her, all there was to know about her body, his body, their bodies meshed as one. They'd be fantastic together, he just knew it. She was trying her wings, this little sparrow, but it would be only with him. He was going to lower her to the blanket and . . .

No! Russell, back off! he warned himself. He had to take it slowly with Annabella so he wouldn't frighten her.

He lifted his head, his breathing rough. "Annabella." He moved his hands to her waist to set her away from him. She didn't budge. He groaned. "Annabella."

She opened her eyes. "Yes?"

"It's time to go in the water and . . . cool off."

"I can't swim."

"I can, and I need to. Right now." He moved his hips against her. "Can you feel that? Can you feel what kissing you, having you close, does to me?"

Her eyes widened.

He smiled. "You're a potent lady, Miss Annabella Abraham."

"Me?"

"You." His smile faded. "You're a beautiful, passionate woman, and a very desirable one. It's time that you realized it, and decided what you're going to do about it."

"Do?"

"I think you're hiding behind frumpy clothes and the facade of a quiet, shy woman who just wants to be left alone to live her life the way she's living it. If I'm wrong and you really want to be left alone, then fine, no problem. Think about it." He pulled her arms from his neck. "I've *got* to get in that water."

Terry turned and sprinted to the edge of the water, then strode into it, striking out moments later with powerful, clean strokes that carried him farther and farther out into the lake.

Annabella's wobbly knees gave up, and she sank to the blanket as she watched the beauty of Terry's strong body cutting through the water.

His words hummed in her mind, teasing her, taunting her, daring her to listen, really listen and hear.

He'd called her beautiful, passionate, desirable. She had to decide if she would allow the woman Terry was convinced was hiding within her to emerge.

That was crazy, she decided. She was Miss Annabella, the librarian, who only attracted men like Ralph Newberry, who just blew his nose, and blew his nose, and . . .

And yet . . .

When Terry Russell had held her, when he had touched her, kissed her, fitted her to his rugged length, she'd registered a sense of something new about herself. And he'd wanted her, he really had, because she'd felt his . . . because his body, pressed hard against hers, had boldly announced that he . . .

"Oh, Annabella," she whispered, "this is frightening." And exciting. But scary. And she didn't know what to do, didn't know who she really was all of a sudden.

She walked to the edge of the water and wiggled her toes in the wet sand as the gentle waves lapped over her feet. She could see Terry in the distance, and at about the middle of the lake he turned and began to swim back, his strokes still steady and powerful.

This swim was just what he'd needed, Terry decided, slicing through the water. Miss Annabella Abraham had tied him up in knots. She'd responded totally to his kiss, and he hadn't wanted it to end. Lord, she felt good nestled against him, and he'd wanted her with a heated ache that was taking an entire lake to cool down.

Without being aware that she was leaving the shore, Annabella went farther into the water, nearly mesmerized by Terry's magnificent performance. She inched onward, her gaze riveted to his tanned arms as they lifted in a hypnotizing rhythm.

Suddenly she gasped as something slithered across

her feet. With a shriek she spun around, kicking at whatever was hiding in the water. In the next instant she realized that she was much farther from shore than she'd intended to go, and now there was nothing under her feet but water.

With a startled shout she sank beneath the surface, then popped up seconds later, sputtering and coughing, her arms flailing as panic gripped her.

"Oh, help!" she yelled. "Help, help!" Then she sank beneath the surface again.

Terry raised his head at the sound of Annabella's cry. He broke the rhythm of his strokes as he saw her sink under the water.

"Lord," he cried, then raced toward her with every ounce of energy he had left in his tiring muscles.

Annabella's head cleared the surface of the water again just as Terry reached her. He scooped her into his arms and stood, the water coming to his shoulders.

"I've got you, Annabella," he said, breathing heavily from his exertion. "Easy. Calm down."

She gasped, then coughed. She flung her arms around his neck and held on for dear life. "I was drowning. I was!"

Terry chuckled and started toward the shore. "Well, not quite, but you got a good mouthful, and a scare. You're all right."

"It was awful. I couldn't stand up and . . ."

"Shh. I have you. Nothing is going to happen to you now."

Annabella buried her face in the crook of Terry's neck and sniffled. He left the water and moved across the sand, glancing down at her as she shivered in his arms. Her breasts were clearly defined beneath the wet, clinging bathing suit, and his gaze lingered there, causing him to stumble slightly. When he came to the blanket, he set her down, then gently pulled her arms from his neck. She was trembling from head to toe as he wrapped a towel around her shoulders.

"Hey," he said, "you're okay. No harm done. Take a deep breath and relax. You're safe, Annabella."

She lifted her head to meet his gaze, and Terry's heart thundered. Oh, man, her eyes were as big as saucers, he thought. She was really frightened. He sat down next to her, circling her shoulders with his arm.

"I—I don't know what happened," she said, her voice shaky. "One minute I was standing there and the next . . . oh, Terry, it was an awful feeling."

"I'm sure it was," he said. "You just sit there until you feel better." He shifted to look at her hair. "The pins are falling out of your hair. I'll see what I can do here." He scooted back a bit and pulled the pins out, watching the heavy, wet braid swing down her back.

Without speaking further, he took the rubber band from the end and slowly and gently combed his fingers through the twisted hair.

"Do you have a brush?" he said.

"In my tote bag, but what—"

"Shh. You just relax." He found the brush and began to draw it through the wet tangles.

Sunlight skittered through the leaves of the trees, casting its glow on them. Terry brushed Annabella's hair in slow, steady strokes, the sun highlighting the different shades of the heavy tresses as they began to dry in thick waves that tumbled to the middle of her back.

Beautiful, Terry mused. Beautiful hair. It was brown, and auburn, and mahogany. It was silky, was made to be touched, made to slide through a man's fingers, then over his body. Incredible hair.

"No one has ever brushed my hair before," Annabella said softly.

"No one? Not even your mother?"

"No."

"You have beautiful hair, Annabella," he said, his voice low. "It really is gorgeous. You should wear it free like this."

"I . . . I don't think so."

Terry turned to sit facing her, his thigh against hers. He lifted handfuls of her hair and watched it slide through his fingers to float over her breasts. His gaze followed the motion, then met hers. She was looking directly at him.

"Beautiful," he said. The silky hair framed her face, softened her features, created the picture of a young, lovely woman. There was no little sparrow in evidence at the moment. There was only Annabella, lovely, lovely Annabella. "So beautiful."

"Thank you for saving my life," she whispered.

"I didn't . . . okay, you're welcome," he said, smiling at her.

And then he leaned forward and kissed her.

The towel slipped from Annabella's shoulders as she raised her hands to sink her fingers into the thick, damp hair on Terry's head. The motion increased the pressure of his mouth on hers, and his tongue plummeted deep within. Without lifting his lips from hers, he laid her back on the blanket, stretching out next to her. The kiss went on and on.

Terry leaned on one forearm as his other hand moved from Annabella's stomach, upward to cup her breast. He drew his thumb over the material of her bathing suit, bringing the nipple to a taut button. He raised his head only long enough to draw air into his lungs, then took possession of her mouth once more. Heat churned within him. Heat and want. Heat, and want, and aching need.

Annabella trembled with desire. When Terry had cupped her breast, she'd nearly purred from the sensual pleasure of what she was experiencing. She'd waited for the feel of his hand on her soft flesh, and now it was there, and it was heaven, even through the material of her bathing suit. And heaven, too, was his mouth on hers, his tongue dueling with hers.

She was kissing and being kissed by the most virile, most handsome, most masculine man she'd ever met. His hand was on her breast, soothing the ache as only he could do. His leg had shifted to trap both of hers in place, and his massive body was half on, half off her.

It was all so wonderful.

A little voice whispered in her mind, and her eyes flew open. It was all taking place in plain view of anyone who might venture by. She, Annabella Abraham, was engaging in . . . what she was engaging in . . . in public! In broad daylight! Merciful saints, she was going to be arrested and thrown in jail. What on earth did she think she was doing?

She slid her hands to Terry's chest and pushed, which was like trying to move a brick wall. She shoved harder.

Terry lifted his head. "What—"he cleared his throat—"what's wrong?"

"Let me up, let me up. This is disgraceful."

"Huh?"

"Terry Russell, move!"

Terry shook his head slightly as if coming out of a trance, then leveled off her and sat up. He drew his knees up to hide the evidence of his arousal, then took a shuddering breath. He looked at Annabella.

She sat up and grabbed the beach towel, holding it in tight fists beneath her chin as she stared straight ahead.

"Annabella," Terry said, his voice gritty with passion, "what is the matter with you?"

She snapped her head around to look at him, her eyes flashing. "You can ask that?"

"Yeah," he said, nodding, "I can. In fact, I just did. What's wrong?"

"Wrong? Oh, nothing, Mr. Russell, nothing at all, except for the fact that I just allowed myself to be . . . be mauled in plain view of . . . of the world!"

"Mauled!" he yelled. "Thanks a helluva lot. I wasn't mauling you, I was kissing you, touching you, and you were enjoying every minute of it, lady. Good Lord, Annabella, no one can see us. I made certain of that."

"Oh, you did, did you?" she said, scrambling to her feet. "You picked this spot on purpose so that you could . . . could have your way with me."

"My way with you?" he repeated, with a burst of

laughter. "I can't believe you said that." Damn, she was fantastic, he thought, looking up at her. Her hair was a wild tumble around her face, her cheeks were flushed, her eyes flashing with anger. The passion he'd felt in her kiss was now exploding in rip-roaring, mad-as-hell emotion. What a sensational woman. "Annabella, calm down."

"No," she said. She picked up her brush and threw it into her tote bag. "I'm mortified by my own behavior." She planted her hands on her hips. "A man can only take what liberties a lady allows him to. I hold myself totally responsible for what took place here."

"Liberties?" Terry said, then hooted with laughter again.

"Shut up, Terry Russell," she hollered. Her bottom lip began to quiver. "I don't know what's happening to me." Her voice trembled and dropped to a whisper. "I've never let any man . . . but then again, it was so wonderful and . . . I'm so confused, because I wanted you to . . . but how would I live with myself if . . ." She burst into tears.

"Oh, Lord," Terry said. He shot to his feet and drew Annabella into the circle of his arms, holding her close as one hand wove through the silken cascade of her hair. "This is all my fault, Annabella. I rushed you, even though I swore to myself that I wouldn't. I'm sorry, I really am. It's just that when I start kissing you, I don't want to stop, and—no, that's no excuse. I'm very, very sorry that I upset you."

Annabella leaned her head on Terry's bare chest, savoring his heat, his strength, his aroma. She sniffled, but made no attempt to move away.

"Annabella?"

"Yes?"

"Do you accept my apology?"

She sighed, then slowly, reluctantly, lifted her head and stepped back, forcing him to drop his arms to his sides.

"It's not your fault," she said. "It's mine."

"No. Look, I wanted to talk to you about that. You know, warn you about guys who might try to seduce you." He paused. "Not that I was trying to seduce you, you understand." He paused again and frowned. "Was I? No, of course not. Nothing is going to happen between us that you're not ready for."

"But I don't know what I'm ready for," she said, throwing up her hands. "Ever since I met you, I've been a befuddled mess. Why are you doing this to me?"

"Not *to* you, Annabella," he said quietly. "*For* you. My father, who cares a great deal about me, urged me to take a good long look at my life. I discovered some things about myself that I didn't know before. I felt, I sensed, that maybe the same could be true with you, that maybe you needed a caring nudge to look at yourself, too. Really look. It was never my intention to make you cry. I'm sorry."

"Why . . . why would you care about me? No one ever has. Not ever."

"I just"—he shrugged—"do. Annabella, if you decide that you prefer your life the way it is, then you might have some answers for me."

"Answers? For you?"

"When I looked deep inside myself, like my father urged me to do, I found that despite my fancy lifestyle, I'm . . . I'm very lonely."

"You? I find that hard to fathom."

"So did I, believe me, but it's true. Thing is, it's not all that easy to find the right person to share your life with, and I had to accept that I might very well spend my life alone. I thought of you, Annabella, and how comfortable you seem existing on your own. I thought I could learn from you how to do that. But then . . ."

"Then?"

"I began to wonder if you might be lonely and not know it. I wanted to do for you what my dad did for me. I wanted you to see more of what life offered before you simply settled for what you have." He raked a hand through his hair. "Damn, spelling it all out like this, I guess I sound pretty arrogant. But believe this, Annabella Abraham, those kisses we shared were real, not part of a master plan. I enjoy kissing you, holding you. So, there it is. If you want to hit me, take your best shot."

Annabella stared at Terry for a long moment, then a soft smile formed on her lips. "Thank you, Terry, for caring. Thank you very much. I have to sort all this through, think about what you said, try to unravel some of this awful confusion in my mind. But I do sincerely thank you for caring, because it has never happened to me before. It's a very warm, very lovely feeling."

He closed the distance between them, then drew his thumb lightly over her lips, then across the dusting of freckles on her nose.

"You're really something, Annabella," he said quietly. "I know you'll do whatever is best for you. I hope so, anyway, because you deserve to be happy."

He smiled. "Would you like to go down to the edge of the water with me and build a sand castle?"

She smiled in return. "I'd love to."

"Good."

Their eyes met and held in a telling moment. A moment of greater understanding and acceptance. A moment separate and apart from the embers of desire still glowing within them.

"Let's go build that castle," Terry said finally. "And, Annabella?"

"Yes?"

"You really do have sensational, absolutely beautiful hair."

She lifted her chin. "Terry, so do you."

He laughed in delight, grabbed her hand, and they headed for the sandy beach, Terry whistling as they went.

They built what they decreed to be the finest castle ever constructed in sand by two people. Together.

Five

The next morning Annabella, wrapped in a fluffy towel, stood in front of her full-length bedroom mirror. She saw that she had a light sunburn which gave her skin a peachy glow without causing her any discomfort.

"Healthy," she said, to her reflection. Yes, she looked healthy and alive, instead of like someone who spent practically every waking hour in a library. It was amazing, she decided, what a little color did for her complexion.

She turned from the mirror and reached in her dresser drawer for her lingerie, feeling exceptionally good. How well she'd slept the previous night. She'd fully expected to toss and turn, thinking about all that Terry had said to her about her life. Instead she'd drifted off to sleep, holding fast to the memories of Terry's kisses.

Now she sank to the edge of the bed and thought

about their conversation. Terry was determined that she should take a closer look at her life, and decide if she was happy or lonely. What he didn't understand was that she had long ago accepted her life as it was.

Annabella sighed. She was who she was. Her life was what it was. She sincerely hoped that Terry found the answers he needed to bring him happiness, but she was accepting her life and herself just as they were.

Annabella got to her feet, made her bed, then turned to open the closet doors. She surveyed her wardrobe, then peered at her peachy complexion in the mirror again. She suddenly decided that if she was going to look healthy for one day of the year, she might as well look . . . healthy.

She pushed the hangers aside and found what she was looking for. It was a pale yellow, polished cotton sundress with a scoop neck, a sash at the waist, and a flared skirt that fell in soft folds. She'd purchased the dress several years before to wear to a garden wedding of a friend in Tulsa and hadn't worn it since.

Shoes, she thought, tapping her chin with her fingertip. She'd worn white accessories to the wedding, and the shoes were white pumps with narrow, two-inch heels. She knew they weren't very practical for work, but the dress wasn't practical, either. Who cared? If she was going to be healthy for a day, she might as well wear the white shoes too.

The dress floated over Annabella's head, the shoes slipped on easily, and a smile formed on her lips when she modelled the outfit in front of the mirror.

She sat down at her vanity and reached for her brush and began arranging her hair in a bun. Suddenly, she stopped and stared into space for a long moment, reliving the memory of Terry brushing her hair so gently after her dunk in the lake.

Finally, she got to her feet, pulled a box of gift wrap and bows from the closet shelf, and found a pale yellow satin ribbon. She brushed her hair until it shone, leaving it soft and full at the sides, and tied the ribbon at the nape of her neck. It was a much more appropriate hairdo for a sundress.

And besides, she thought with a shrug, no one would notice her hair or her dress or the fact that she looked healthy for a day. No one noticed Annabella Abraham.

The Harmony Public Library was housed in an old building that had once been the city jail. There had been no librarian during the five years prior to Annabella's arrival, because the woman who once held the position had eloped with the milkman, and neither had been heard from since. As librarian, Annabella had inherited a dark, dusty building with no particular order or system for housing the books. In the three years since accepting the position, she had transformed the library into a bright, cheery place and had properly cataloged all the books and placed them on the shelves in exact order. The city council had allotted her a budget, and she spent it wisely on equipment, supplies, and the continuing purchase of carefully selected new books.

The library soon became a popular place for an

outing in Harmony, to the point where Annabella needed help keeping the facility running smoothly. Mrs. Perdy, a widow in her seventies, became Annabella's part-time assistant.

And it was Mrs. Perdy who greeted Annabella when she entered the library.

"Good morning," Mrs. Perdy said. "How are you today, Miss . . . land's sake, would you look at you? Now, don't you just look as pretty as a spring flower?"

"Oh, well, I . . ." Annabella started, feeling a warm flush on her already healthy cheeks.

"Mercy, mercy, mercy," Mrs. Perdy said, beaming as she scrutinized Annabella from head to toe, "I hardly know what to say. You're pretty as a picture, Miss Annabella, like a yellow daffodil. Well, I just had no idea that you . . . land's sake, wonders never cease."

"Really, Mrs. Perdy," Annabella said, trying to edge around the stout woman, "it's just a sundress. There's no cause to make such a fuss."

"There certainly is cause, young lady. I never did understand why you always wore those old-lady clothes and old-lady colors. And your hair. Why, it's lovely! There's a glow about you too."

"I'm sunburned," Annabella muttered, hurrying toward her little office.

Mrs. Perdy was right behind her. "You can tell me, Miss Annabella, and it won't go past my lips. Have you decided to go stepping out with Ralph Newberry?"

Annabella stopped so quickly she nearly fell out of her shoes, and Mrs. Perdy came close to bumping into her. Annabella turned around.

"No, Mrs. Perdy," she said sternly, "I have no intention of stepping out, as you put it, with Mr. Newberry."

"Praise the Lord for that," Mrs. Perdy said. "I, for one, couldn't tolerate a man who does nothing more than blow his nose."

Annabella couldn't help laughing as she went into her office. Mrs. Perdy hovered in the doorway.

"So?" Mrs. Perdy asked. "Who is he, then? What man put you in a mind to get all gussied up and looking like a spring flower?"

"Really, Mrs. Perdy," Annabella said, lifting her chin, "why would you think there's a man behind the fact that I decided to wear a sundress today? You're making a very big hoopla over a very little dress."

"It's a man, all right," Mrs. Perdy said, starting away. "I'd bet my bingo money on it. I'll figure out who it is. Heaven knows there aren't that many to pick from in Harmony. Now, let's see . . ."

"Oh, for Pete's sake," Annabella said, shaking her head. She'd worn the dress to show off her healthy, glowing complexion, she thought. Mrs. Perdy had been watching soap operas too long. A dress was a dress. And besides, Terry would have no reason to come into the library to . . . what? "What?" she repeated out loud.

Annabella sank into the chair at her desk and blinked. Where on earth had that thought come from? she asked herself. She knew why she'd worn the sundress, and it had nothing whatsoever to do with Mr. Terry Russell.

In fact, she doubted that she'd see Terry again while he was home on vacation. They'd had a lovely outing . . . a wonderful, memory-filled outing. Terry had expressed his caring concern for her future happiness, and that was that. The sundress, darn it, had nothing to do with him.

Annabella got to her feet, then smoothed the skirt of the dress. She looked like a spring flower? she pondered. A daffodil? Pretty as a picture? Oh, she did not. Enough of this nonsense. She had work to do.

In the middle of the afternoon Terry stopped in at the small café where he and his friends had spent hours as teenagers. Little had changed. The tables were still scarred, the leather booths were dry and cracked, the odor of grease hung in the air.

Terry smiled, recalling his cocky youth and the endless flirting, laughing, and talking that had taken place in the old café. Gussie, the waitress, was older now, but Terry didn't doubt for a minute that she still kept the teenagers in line, just as she had in his day. Gussie's elbows were propped on the counter and her nose was buried in a book.

"Hey, Gussie," he asked, "are you in there?"

She straightened and smiled. "Terry Russell, you handsome so-and-so. I heard tell you were home to see your folks. I wondered if you were going to come by to visit your old Gussie."

"Wouldn't have missed it." He swung his leg over a red stool and sat down.

"Cherry cola?" Gussie asked.

"You bet. You still remember my favorite drink."

"You were my favorite boy," she said, reaching for a glass.

"What are you reading?"

"A murder mystery. I love them and I'm darned good at figuring out who done it too. Miss Annabella has a whole section of mysteries over at the library. She gets new ones in all the time too. I was over there early this morning and checked this one out. The gardener did it, I'm sure of it. Here's your soda."

"Thanks, Gussie."

"I must say, I was mighty surprised when I saw Miss Annabella this morning."

Terry halted the glass halfway to his mouth. "Oh?" he said, then took a swallow of the drink.

"I hardly recognized her at first. My stars, she looked so . . . so . . ."

Terry leaned forward. "So?"

"Pretty. She's wearing a yellow sundress, can you imagine that? Miss Annabella in a yellow sundress? And her hair is tied with a yellow ribbon. I had no idea she had such pretty hair. I told her I thought she looked as fresh and nice as a sunny day."

"What did she say to that?" Terry asked.

"She smiled and thanked me for the compliment. You know, I can't remember ever stopping to speak to Miss Annabella before, other than to say greetings as I was checking my books in and out. Mrs. Perdy pulled me aside and said she just knows there's a man behind Miss Annabella's looking so fine today. And, Mrs. Perdy said, it's not that Ralph Newberry and his runny nose. Anyway, a few other folks commented on Miss Annabella when they came in here today. Everyone just can't get over her wearing that yellow sundress."

"Interesting," Terry said, then quickly drained his glass. He stood and put some money on the counter. "Good to see you, Gussie."

"Fine seeing you, Terry. Lordy, you did grow up to be a handsome devil. It's time you married again, settled down, had a baby or two."

"Yeah, I think you're right," he said. "See you later."

Terry covered the few blocks to the library with long strides. He entered the old building and glanced around, not seeing Annabella but immediately aware of the bright, cheerful atmosphere she'd created in the library. He saw Ralph Newberry sitting at a table reading a book and dabbing at his nose with a tissue. Terry frowned and went to the counter just as Annabella came out of her office.

Look at her, he thought. She looks beautiful.

Annabella stopped as she saw Terry at the counter. She gave her heart a firm directive to cease its suddenly wild beating and she met Terry's gaze.

"Hello, Terry," she said quietly as she walked up to the counter.

Oh, damn, that voice, he thought. There were times when he just couldn't handle the sultry, sexy sound of her voice.

"Annabella," he said, nodding. "You're looking very special today."

"Thank you."

"Why?" he asked, frowning.

"Why? Well, saying 'Thank you' is an appropriate reply to a compliment."

"No, why are you wearing that dress?" he asked, his frown deepening.

"Because I wanted to. Why are you looking so cross?"

"Why did you want to wear the dress, and your hair like that, and high-heeled shoes? Am I supposed to be getting a message here?"

"Message?"

"Yeah, you know, you've decided to broaden your horizons, break out of your mold. I see your buddy Ralph Newberry is here blowing his nose."

"Terry, lower your voice," Annabella said. "I don't understand why you're so angry. Why are you behaving this way?"

"I don't know," he said, throwing up his hands. "I guess maybe I thought you'd tell me, talk it over, before you started making changes in your life."

"I'm not making changes in my life," she said in a loud whisper.

"What would you call that dress?" he yelled. Ralph Newberry jumped in his chair and dropped his book. "Well?"

"Hush," Annabella hissed. "Just hush."

Mrs. Perdy came out of the office. "I'm on my way home, Miss Annabella. Time for my soap operas, you know. Well, Terry Russell, as I live and breathe." She looked at Annabella, back to Terry, then smiled. "Ah-h-h, now it all makes sense."

"Oh, please," Annabella said, rolling her eyes to the heavens.

"Isn't she just as pretty as a picture, Terry?" Mrs. Perdy cooed. "I knew there was a man behind the wearing of that dress. I may be old, but I'm sharp as a tack. Y'all have a fine evening." She hurried away.

Annabella planted her hands flat on the counter, leaned toward Terry, and glared. "Now see what you've done?" she whispered.

He put his hand on his chest. "Me?" He smiled, a hundred-watt, dazzling smile. "I never said a thing to Mrs. Perdy. Not a word passed my lips, Miss Annabella."

"You know how she is," Annabella said. "She sees a potential soap opera wherever she looks. She thinks that you and I, that we're, that I wore this dress because . . ."

"Really?" Terry said, raising his eyebrows and oozing innocence. "And just why *did* you wear that dress, Annabella?"

"Because I wanted to!" she shrieked.

The next instant she clamped her hand over her mouth in wide-eyed horror.

Ralph Newberry got to his feet and hurried to the door.

"Nice seeing you, Ralph," Terry said, over his shoulder. "Hope your allergies get better."

"Oh-h-h, you're a menace," Annabella said, then spun around and marched into her office.

Terry chuckled, then glanced around the library, seeing that no one else was there. He strolled behind the counter and into Annabella's office. She was standing by her desk, straightening a stack of already neat papers.

"I know you're there, Terry Russell," she said tightly, "but I'm not acknowledging your presence. I have never, ever, raised my voice in a library before. That was disgraceful."

"Indeed it was," he said. He moved to stand right behind her. "It wasn't behavior befitting a prim and proper librarian, that's for sure." He paused. "Oh, I forgot, you're not acknowledging my presence. You don't mind if I acknowledge *your* presence, do you?" He filled his hands with the luxurious mane of her hair. "Lord, I love your hair."

Annabella stiffened, then turned quickly to face him, her eyes flashing. "Stop that," she said. Oh, he was so close she could feel the heat from his body, could smell a woodsy after-shave and an aroma that was uniquely his.

"Why did you wear the dress, Annabella?" Terry said, his voice low.

She looked up into his eyes. "Because I was sunburned, and looked healthy for a day, and it seemed like a good idea at the time." She stopped speaking as she realized there was no more air left in her lungs.

"I see," he said, lifting his hands to frame her face. "Are you sure you aren't beginning to make changes in yourself?"

"No," she whispered. "I thought about it and . . . no."

Annabella's words were smothered by Terry's mouth melting over hers. Her lashes drifted down, her arms slid around his waist, and her tongue met his eagerly, tasting, savoring.

So, so sweet, Terry thought, drawing Annabella closer to his body. So soft. And she smelled so good. But why was it so important that she'd worn that dress for him? Why the rush of panic when she'd said she wasn't planning on making any changes in her life? If she didn't make changes, there'd be no room for him. So? But—ah, hell, he couldn't think straight when he was kissing this woman.

The kiss deepened. The room faded into oblivion. There were only the two of them and the desire that churned within them. There was only feel, and taste, and aroma, and want—heavy, throbbing, heated, aching want.

Terry tore his mouth from Annabella's and drew a ragged breath. His heart thundered in his chest, and his arousal was straining against the zipper of his jeans.

"Oh, my," Annabella whispered, slowly opening her eyes.

"Oh, my," Terry repeated. "What are you doing to me, Annabella Abraham?"

"I don't understand what you're doing to me, either, Terry. I think—I think it might be best if you just stayed away from me."

"The hell I will," he roared.

"Hush. This is a library."

"Well, don't give me this garbage about staying away from you." He raked a hand through his hair. "And another thing," he said, none too quietly. Annabella jumped. "You're playing mind games with yourself, lady. You can tell me from here to Sunday that you haven't decided to change your life, and I won't believe you. Why? Because you're standing there in that dress, that's why."

"But I told you that I wore it because—"

"Cut," he said, slicing his hand through the air

for silence. "Would you go out to dinner with me tonight?"

"What?" she said, obviously confused by his sudden change of topic.

"Dinner. We'll go to the Carriage House, between here and Castle Cove. I'll pick you up at seven."

"Oh, well, I don't—"

"Dammit, Annabella, just say yes before I slip right over the edge here."

She blinked. "Yes."

"Good," he said, then started toward the door. "And wear that dress," he added before he disappeared. "For me!"

"Certainly," Annabella said to the empty room, waving her hand breezily in the air.

She swallowed a rather hysterical bubble of laughter, then sank into her chair and pressed her hands to her cheeks.

Terry thought *he* was slipping over the edge? she mused. He ought to try *her* befuddled brain on for size. She was so confused. Except for one thing, she admitted. She did, indeed, enjoy being held and kissed by Terry Russell. The desire within her grew stronger each time he took her into his arms. She could conjure up a romantic fantasy about Terry making love to her that would shock Clara and Susie. Oh, heavenly days, Annabella thought, what was she going to do?

By the time Terry had walked home, poured himself a glass of lemonade, and settled into the porch swing, he'd decided that he was certifiably insane.

Annabella had the right to make her own choices, he knew that. She could decide to maintain her limited life-style, he knew that. His part in all of this was to point out her options to her, then step back and quietly see what she would do. Dammit, he knew that!

Then why was he so determined to convince her that she *was* making changes in her life, changes that included him? He didn't want to hear, refused to listen to, any hint that she'd decided to continue on with the life she'd had before he'd met her. He wanted her to grow, to make room for him. But that was nuts. He was only here on vacation, would be leaving soon. His behavior made no sense at all.

Mike Russell came out onto the porch. "You look like a storm about to rumble," he said to Terry.

"Women drive me crazy," Terry said moodily, then drained his glass.

"Women in general, or one in particular?" Mike asked, settling into the recliner.

"Well, hell, don't you think that wearing a yellow sundress is significant?"

Mike chuckled. "Depends on who's wearing it. If you showed up in a yellow sundress, I'd definitely find it significant."

"Give me a break, Dad. This is serious business. Why would she wear that dress, and still claim she wasn't making any changes in her life? Answer me that."

"I—"

"I'll tell you why," Terry went on. "Because she's too afraid to admit even to herself that she's doing it, so she came up with the healthy sunburn bull."

"This certainly is a fascinating conversation," Mike muttered, shaking his head slightly.

"Or am I kidding myself?" Terry said dismally. "For all I know, she really means it when she says she isn't going to change."

"Could be," Mike said, then shrugged in total confusion.

"That's hard to believe," Terry said, "it really is. I can see the changes. Or am I only seeing what I want to see? Damn it all, she's really driving me crazy."

"That part is coming across loud and clear, Son."

Mary Russell stepped out onto the porch. "Terry, you have several messages by the phone. Some of those pilots and other people you contacted are returning your calls."

"Yeah, okay, thanks," he said, getting to his feet. "I'll call them back right now. Oh, by the way, I won't be home for dinner. That is, if I can borrow—"

"The car," Mike said. "Sure thing."

"You're eating out?" Mary said.

"Yeah, at the Carriage House."

"Oh, how nice," Mary said. "That's such a quaint restaurant. Who are you going with?"

"A woman in a yellow sundress," Mike said, "who is robbing Terry of his sanity."

Mary's brows rose. "Pardon me?"

"Miss Annabella Abraham," Mike said, smiling smugly. "It took me a while, but I figured out the conversation Terry and I just had."

"You're taking Miss Annabella to dinner?" Mary asked, smiling. "I think that's splendid."

America's most popular, most compelling romance novels...

Here, at last...love stories that really involve you! Fresh, finely crafted novels with story lines so believable you'll feel you're actually living them! Characters you can relate to...exciting places to visit...unexpected plot twists...all in all, exciting romances that satisfy your mind and delight your heart.

Get one full-length Loveswept FREE every month!
Now you can be sure you'll never, ever miss a single
Loveswept title by enrolling in our special reader's home
delivery service. A service that will bring you all six new
Loveswept romances each month for the price of five—and
deliver them to you before they appear in the bookstores!

Examine 6 Loveswept Novels for

15 days FREE!

(SEE OTHER SIDE FOR DETAILS)

"It might be, if I don't wring her neck," Terry said, then strode into the house.

"Pardon me?" Mary asked again.

Mike just laughed.

The first call that Terry returned was to Houston Tyler. Houston was the husband of January St. John Tyler of St. John Enterprises, where Terry worked. Terry had been the best man at January and Houston's wedding, which had been held at January Hall, the Tyler's home on an island off of the coast of Maine. Terry knew that Houston and January had a very happy marriage. They'd overcome the differences in their backgrounds, Houston being a blue-collar construction worker, in contrast to January, who came from an extremely wealthy family. January and Houston now had a beautiful baby girl named Julie.

When Terry reached his friend, Houston said he'd contacted several of the executives of St. John Enterprises, and two were interested in the Cessna. They would decide within the next few days if they wished to go further and arrange to test-fly the airplane.

"I appreciate your help, Houston," Terry said.

"No problem. We'll see what happens. These guys like to hunt and can visualize hopping around in the plane to various choice hunting spots. So, how's the vacation going?"

"Fine."

"Must be nice to be home. I know how I feel when all the Tylers and spouses get together. It's great."

"Yeah, great."

"What's wrong, buddy?" Houston said. "You don't sound like your usual chipper self."

"Houston, you've been married awhile now. Do you feel you understand women?"

Houston laughed. "Are you bonkers, man? I will never understand women. I love January, but she knows full well that I don't understand her half of the time. Now I've got a baby girl I probably won't understand either."

"That's rough," Terry said, frowning.

"Hell, no. You're misinterpreting what I'm saying because I'm definitely not complaining. Okay, here's an example. I was late getting to the island one night last week because I got tied up on a construction site. Not only was I late, but I'd totally forgotten we were having company for dinner."

"Deep trouble," Terry said.

"You'd think so, wouldn't you? I came slopping in muddy, sweaty, and there was everyone dressed to the teeth and already eating dessert. I figured I was a dead man."

"Guaranteed."

"What can I say? January jumped up from the table, flung her arms around my neck, and said she'd been so worried about me. She didn't care that she'd gotten mud all over her dress, only that I'd eat the dinner she'd saved for me. Understand her, my man? Never. Love her? Until the day I die." He paused. "You've got woman trouble, huh?"

"In spades," Terry said. "If only I could understand why she—"

"Weren't you listening, pal? You *can't* understand

'em. All you can do is figure out how *you* feel, then sit back and wait for the surprises. Just go with the flow, Terry."

"Figure out how *I* feel?"

"Yes, because I'm telling you this. I know you were married before, but you're older now, different. This is a whole new ball game. Forget trying to understand this woman, Terry. Just concentrate on where you're coming from."

"Oh."

"Good luck, Terry ole boy," Houston said, chuckling.

"I think I'm going to need all the luck I can get. My brain is turning into oatmeal."

"Sounds about right. Hundred-pound women can wipe out two-hundred-pound men without breaking stride. Well, I'll be in touch about the plane."

"Thanks, Houston, for the advice," Terry said, then slowly replaced the receiver. Well, he thought, that had certainly been informative. Instead of trying to figure out Annabella, he should be zeroing in on himself for now.

How did he really feel about Annabella Abraham?

Good question, he admitted. Trouble was, he had no idea what he would do with the answer.

Six

Terry Russell had a plan.

He was whistling as he knotted a paisley tie over a pale blue shirt, then shrugged into the blue blazer he wore over gray slacks.

It was a great plan, he told himself. Houston had said that Terry shouldn't attempt to understand Annabella. According to Houston, Terry's concentration should be centered on himself, and his feelings for Annabella. Fine. But he was taking Houston's line of thinking one step farther.

As he drove to Annabella's, Terry reviewed the brilliant logic of his plan. If he was to learn his true feelings regarding his sudden and strong attraction for Annabella, then it seemed only fair and fitting that she should discover what she was feeling for him.

Maybe the strong effect they had on each other was strictly physical, Terry mused. But maybe it was more. They owed it to themselves to find the answers. And so he'd execute his plan. Annabella *had* to stay available, couldn't jump back into the protective nest of the little brown sparrow where Terry wouldn't be able to reach her.

He was totally convinced that Annabella liked the changes taking place in her life—liked him, his touches and kisses. But she was frightened, and ready to cut and run because so much had happened so quickly. Well, he thought, she wasn't going to run. She hadn't given him enough time.

"Great plan," Terry said to himself as he pulled into Annabella's driveway. Now convincing Annabella not to retreat to her old life-style would be the tough part, he thought dryly. There was a lot of spunk, stubbornness, and feisty determination beginning to surface in Annabella. And, the passion—it grew stronger each time he took her into his arms. She was really something, this Annabella Abraham.

Annabella Abraham had a plan.

After freshening up, rebrushing her hair, and tying it with the yellow satin ribbon, she'd had a chance to relax and calm her jangled nerves. While sitting in her quiet living room, she reviewed the events of the day, especially Terry's reaction to her wearing the yellow sundress.

She had worn the dress, Annabella thought decisively, for the sole purpose of appearing healthy for a day with her sunburn. That was it. It had nothing to do with Terry or his urging her to consider the possibility of making changes in her life.

Each time she pictured making any changes, breaking out of her well-ordered existence, she saw herself doing so with Terry. She envisioned herself being held and kissed by Terry Russell. She allowed herself fleeting romantic fantasies of making love with him. She relived the hours at the lake spent in his company and fantasized about the evening ahead at the lovely restaurant. Oh, indeed, they were changes, but they weren't just Annabella changes, they were centered on the two of them being together. And that was very, very wrong.

Annabella realized that Terry was only home on vacation. He was a temporary addition to her life and would soon be gone. She would be left behind to work in the library, go to the Quilting Club, and make sugar tea-cookies for the church bake sales. Nothing would be different. Life would go on as it had before. Quite simply, that was the way things were. She was Annabella Abraham, the librarian in Harmony, Oklahoma, and she was alone.

Annabella sighed. She assured herself she wasn't feeling sorry for herself. She was merely accepting facts as they were and had always been. She lived a quiet, orderly existence which varied little from one day to the next, and that was fine. She was content. She was happy. But then again . . . no, no, her life was very satisfactory just as it was.

But she did have a plan.

It was daring and bold, and very unlike herself, but she was going to do it. Terry was convinced that she was making major changes in her life and seemed determined that she recognize and acknowledge them. Why he was so set upon making her admit that, she had no idea.

What she did know was that while Terry Russell was in Harmony, she was going to give the impression that she was, indeed, becoming a new Annabella Abraham. For a handful of days, a stolen number of hours, she was going to bask in Terry's attention, be held, touched, and kissed by him. She was going to step out of herself and be something and someone she wasn't, then cherish the memories of it all when he was gone.

It wasn't quite honest, she realized that, but her actions would hurt no one. Terry would leave, she would return to being who she really was, and the memories would be hers. The changes would be temporary, just as Terry's emergence into her life was, and when it was over things would go back to the way they had been. It was a gift to herself. It was being what Terry wanted her to be, so that she could be a part of his life for a short period of time.

Oh, yes, Annabella mused, it was a daring and bold plan, but one she had every intention of carrying out. Be it right or wrong, she was going to do it.

She heard the sound of a car in the driveway and took a steadying breath. Heavens, she thought, she was terribly nervous. Well, she had just cause. She was about to start playing a role, something she'd never done before in her life. She had to keep telling herself that no one could be hurt by her deception, for that was very true. She just wanted some memories of when she'd been half of a whole, part of a pair. Memories of Annabella and Terry. Together.

A knock sounded at the door. Annabella took another deep breath, then went to answer it.

The plan, she thought dramatically, had begun!

She opened the door.

She opened her mouth to greet Terry, but nothing came out except a tiny puff of air that carried a rather weak "Oh" with it. He was, she thought hazily, so handsome in those clothes. Just overwhelmingly gorgeous.

"Hello, Annabella," Terry said, looking directly into her eyes. Beautiful, he thought. "May . . . um . . . I come in?"

"What?" Annabella blinked, snapping herself out of her semi-trance. "Oh, yes, of course." She stepped back. "You look very nice."

"Thank you, so do you. And thank you for wearing the dress, and your hair like that. Are you ready to go?"

"Certainly. I'll just get my purse." She picked it up off the end table. "I have my purse now, so I'm ready to go." She smiled brightly.

Terry frowned. "Are you all right?"

"Me? Oh, yes, I'm fine, splendid. I'm . . . I'm hungry. I didn't have time for lunch today. My, my, yes, I'm starving. That's what I am, all right—hungry as a bear."

"I see," Terry said, nodding slowly. "Well, then, we'd better go feed you."

"Good idea," she said, then swooshed out the door.

Terry followed her. Was she acting weird or was it his imagination? Maybe she was nervous. She had a dinner date, was wearing a different dress, her hair was flowing down her back. Well, she was going to relax and have a great time. He hoped. Yes, dammit, she would!

During the drive to the Carriage House, Terry asked Annabella what she thought of a popular author who was sweeping the best-seller lists with her series of romantic intrigue novels.

Brilliant, he thought smugly. She was chattering like a magpie and her eyes were sparkling. Bringing up the subject of books was an absolutely brilliant move on his part. He amazed himself at times with his intelligence.

The Carriage House was a rustic old building that had been carefully decorated to maintain an atmosphere of charm and coziness. It had a reputation for having excellent prime rib, which both Annabella and Terry ordered.

Terry selected a wine, then continued to steer the conversation toward subjects he felt Annabella would be responsive to. He brought her up to date on his progress in trying to sell the Cessna, and Annabella thanked him again for his help.

"It's a great little plane," he said.

"If you like airplanes," she said, smiling.

Their food was served and they ate in silence for several minutes.

"Why are you so frightened of flying?" Terry asked finally. "You said the day we met that you've never flown. Did someone you know have a bad experience? A rough, bumpy flight or something?"

"No, nothing like that. And, yes, I've never flown. I wouldn't have had anywhere to go. It's just the whole idea of being so far off the ground inside a plane and not being able to get out if something went wrong."

"But you've never tried it. You can't judge flying unless you've given it a try. It's like anything else new you undertake, you can't be too quick to pass judgment." Slick, Russell, he thought. He was shifting the conversation exactly where he wanted it to go. "Understand?"

"I guess so," she said, shrugging. "This dinner is delicious."

"Very good. Annabella, I want to talk to you."

"We *are* talking."

"I mean about a specific thing. Okay?"

"Certainly."

He couldn't, wouldn't, blow this! "Annabella, I'm very aware that you didn't want to admit why you wore that dress today."

"I—"

"No, wait," he said, raising his hand. "Just listen for a minute."

"Yes, all right. I'm sorry that I interrupted you. That wasn't courteous of me. Please go on."

"Right. Look, I understand that making changes in one's life is no small thing, and could very well be frightening. It could be tempting to go on as always rather than facing the unknowns."

Terry paused, waiting to see if Annabella wanted to comment. She took another bite of her salad, then looked at him again, an unreadable expression on her face.

"The point I'm trying to make here is," Terry went on, "that by denying that you're making changes in your life, you'll end up not making any. That wouldn't be fair to yourself, or to me, Annabella. We enjoy being together. And unless you admit that you're changing, there won't be any room in your life for me."

Oh, Lord, he thought, was this making sense? He felt like a blithering idiot. He couldn't read her reaction at all. She just kept eating, and looking at him blankly.

"Therefore," he said, feeling a trickle of sweat run down his back, "I'm asking you to give this, give us, a chance. I'm asking that you admit that you've made some changes, and agree to make more as they come to your mind. There are questions emerging here that need answers, and we have the right to find those answers. Don't run back to your old way of living without giving this a fair trial. Go with the changes, with whatever feels right."

Annabella smiled. "Okay. May I have the salt, please?"

"What?" he said, leaning toward her.

"The salt. It's there by your elbow."

He picked up the saltshaker and handed it to her.

"You said 'Okay' a second ago," he said. "What does that mean?"

She shrugged. "It means 'Okay,' that I'll do as you asked."

"Spell it out for me."

"You don't remember what you said?"

"I want to be sure we're on the same wavelength, Annabella."

They certainly were, she thought. It was as though he'd read her mind. What Terry didn't know was that the changes would be temporary, the means by which to gather her precious, precious memories.

"Annabella?"

"What? Oh. Well, I'm agreeing that I've made changes, and that I'll make more as the occasions arise. It may be frightening, but I won't run from any of this. I'll be brave, courageous, and bold . . . or whatever."

Terry slouched back in his chair. "I'll be damned."

"May I have the pepper now, please? It's by your other elbow. Terry, your mouth is open."

He handed her the pepper. "I can't believe you agreed to this so easily. I thought it would take all evening to convince you that I'm right. This is fantastic, Annabella. We're going to have the time we need."

To gather memories, Annabella thought. Oh, dear, her conscience was niggling at her. Terry looked so pleased, and there she sat, knowing she was simply acting out a role—a fantasy. No, she mustn't back down now. He'd be leaving soon. He wouldn't be hurt by this, wouldn't lose anything, and she had so many lovely memories to gain.

"Thank you, Annabella," Terry said quietly. "Thank you very much."

Their gazes met and held, and Annabella couldn't speak. The warmth and tenderness in Terry's blue eyes made her heart skip a beat, then begin again in a racing tempo. Desire swirled within her, and she wondered what might be showing in her eyes.

She wanted him to kiss her, now, right now, hold her close to his rugged body, wrap her in the heat and strength of his strong arms.

She wanted Terry Russell to make love to her. She wanted it very much.

Good Lord, Terry thought, Annabella's eyes were turning him inside out. He wondered if anyone would notice if he leaped across the table and kissed her senseless? Then he'd carry her out of this restaurant to a secluded, private place and make love to her until dawn. Annabella. Beautiful Annabella. She had agreed to his plan, and he was going to be there every step of the way. Oh, those eyes. If she said one word to him right now in that sexy, sultry voice of hers, he'd be a goner.

"Terry?"

He plunked his elbow on the table and dropped his forehead to the palm of his hand.

Annabella's eyes widened. "Terry? My goodness, what's wrong?"

He lifted his head and managed a weak smile. "Nothing. Really."

"But—"

"Would you care for dessert?" the waiter asked, suddenly appearing at their table.

Bless you, Terry thought, looking up at the man.

"I believe I'll have a dish of raspberry sherbet, please," Annabella said.

"And you, sir?" the waiter said to Terry.

"Cake. Any kind. Chocolate if you have it. Yes, chocolate."

"Very good," the waiter said. "Coffee?"

"Decaffeinated, please," Annabella said.

"The same," Terry said. The waiter moved away. Terry looked at Annabella. "So, you like raspberry sherbet," he said, a bit too loudly. "That's nice. One of those interesting little tidbits people learn about each other when they . . . forget it," he said, shaking his head slightly.

"Terry, you're acting very strangely all of a sudden."

The waiter returned with their desserts, and Terry decided the guy deserved a medal for his timing.

"Dig right into that raspberry sherbet, Annabella," Terry said as the waiter walked away, "and I'll eat my chocolate cake. Well, now, it even has chocolate frosting. How about that?"

"Mr. Russell, what is your problem?" Annabella asked frowning.

Terry leaned forward, trapped her hand with his on top of the table, and spoke in a raspy whisper. "I'll tell you my problem, Miss Abraham. When you look at me with your great big brown eyes, then speak in that incredibly sexy voice of yours, I can't always handle it. This is one of those times."

"Sexy voice?" Annabella said, more in the form of a squeak.

"Damned right, lady. That's part of it, you know. The fact that you have no idea how beautiful you are, how expressive your eyes are. And your voice? It makes me want you. Want to make love to you, Annabella Abraham."

"Oh, dear," she said, her free hand holding her heart. "You can't say that here, in this public place."

He narrowed his eyes. "I just said it."

"Yes. Well, you did, didn't you?" She paused, then smiled. "Sexy voice?"

A startled expression crossed Terry's face, then he chuckled and moved back, releasing her hand.

"A sexy, sultry, tie-me-in-knots voice," he said,

grinning. "Hey, have you forgotten your spiel about my trying to have my way with you? I just told you I wanted you, and I said it in a restaurant to boot."

Annabella merely nodded. She took a bite of sherbet. "Mmm, delicious. Anyway, about what you said. It seems to me that this is a free country, and you have the right to say just about anything you want to."

Terry halted his forkful of chocolate cake halfway to his mouth. "You're kidding."

"Not at all," Annabella said pleasantly. "I mean, I could say that I wanted you, and wanted you to make love to me if I felt so inclined."

"Do you? Feel so inclined?" he asked, leaning slightly toward her.

"Well, yes."

The cake fell off Terry's fork and landed on the tablecloth in a gooey lump.

"You do?" he croaked.

Annabella took another bite of sherbet and nodded while her mouth was full. "This is so tasty. Now, where was I?"

"Feeling inclined," he prompted, ignoring the chocolate mess on the tablecloth.

"Oh, yes. Well, you see, there's a tremendous difference between saying and doing. I could *say* I'd like to rob a bank, but that doesn't mean I would actually *do* it."

"Annabella, there is no comparison between making love and robbing a bank."

She shrugged. "I suppose not. I was simply making a point."

"You haven't ever—well, you haven't, have you?"

"Robbed a bank?"

"No! Made love," he said. "Been with a man."

She frowned. "Is that an appropriate question to ask a lady?"

"I have no idea, but it's important, so I'm asking it. Actually, I already know the answer."

"You do?"

"I do. Are you waiting for your wedding night?" He shook his head. "I can't believe I'm taking part in this conversation. No one waits for their wedding night." He paused. "Well, maybe that isn't true. You're a definite candidate for waiting for your wedding night. Are you? Waiting?"

"I don't think so," she said, squinting her eyes in concentration. "I . . . no, I'm not."

"Why not?"

"Because I don't anticipate having a wedding night. Aren't you going to eat your cake?"

He glanced at the glob on the tablecloth. "No. Don't you want a husband, a home, children?"

Yes! "What we want and what we receive do not always match. You said yourself that you might spend your future alone, even though it wouldn't be by choice."

He nodded. "Of course, a person can't just sit back and wait to be handed what he wants on a silver platter. Sometimes we have to go after it, fight for it, not give up."

"And sometimes," she said quietly, "that doesn't make any difference, and the outcome will still be the same. We have to accept what we have and get on with our lives."

"But you've agreed to make some changes in your life, Annabella. You're not forgetting that, are you?"

"No, I'm not forgetting," she said. Temporary changes. Memory-making changes. Just for a little while. "I assure you that I haven't forgotten."

"Good."

Annabella concentrated on her sherbet, giving it much more attention than it deserved, but wishing to avert her eyes from Terry's scrutiny. She recalled how he'd said she had expressive eyes, and she didn't want to run the risk of his seeing any clue that she wasn't being completely honest.

Expressive eyes, she repeated his words to herself. Her? And a sexy, sultry voice? Her? Imagine that. And imagine Miss Annabella Abraham sitting in a restaurant with an extremely handsome man, discussing whether or not she was saving herself, her virtue, her virginity, for her wedding night. How mortifying.

No, it wasn't, she thought in the next instant. She hadn't been embarrassed at all, now that she looked back on the conversation. It had been an open, honest sharing of values and viewpoints. It had been more than a sexual discussion, it had been two . . . friends, yes, friends, giving glimpses to more of themselves. She'd never had a really close friend with whom she could share her innermost thoughts and feelings. Had Terry Russell become her friend?

Well, she mused, she'd always heard that one's lover, the person one loved, should also be one's best friend. Lover? The person one loved? Terry? Oh, Annabella, just eat, she ordered herself.

Terry sat back in his chair, crossed his arms loosely

over his chest, and watched Annabella attack her dessert as though she hadn't eaten in three days.

His mind raced. He knew she wanted him, and wanted to make love with him. What he'd felt in her ever-increasing responses to his kisses, she'd now said in words. Comparing it to robbing a bank wasn't the most romantic or flattering thing he'd ever heard, but she did want to make love with him.

Terry ran his hand over his chin and squinted his eyes at Annabella, wishing he could peer into her mind. Annabella was a virgin. How could he even consider being the one to—but she was an adult, a twenty-nine-year-old woman, who was perfectly capable of making her own decisions and choices. He wouldn't seduce her, but if making love with him was what she wanted, then . . . oh, hell, he was losing his mind again.

"That," Annabella said, bringing Terry from his jumbled thoughts, "was marvelous sherbet. The dinner was delicious too. Thank you, Terry."

"It was my pleasure. Would you like to have lunch with me tomorrow at Gussie's?"

"Tomorrow? Oh, well, you see, I planned to call Mrs. Perdy in the morning and ask her if she could work the full day. If she can't, or won't because of her soap operas, she can close the library early. It won't make that big a difference. Ralph Newberry will just have to find somewhere else to spend his afternoon."

"Oh? And where will you be?"

"I have a great deal of vacation and sick leave I haven't used. I'm going to Tulsa tomorrow."

"May I ask why?"

"I'm going shopping for some new clothes."

Terry leaned forward in his chair and crossed his arms on the table. "No joke?"

Annabella laughed. "Well, I sound very confident at the moment, but I may lose my nerve once I get there."

"I'll go with you."

"Pardon me?"

"Think about it, Annabella. You're going to be trying new styles and colors. Don't you think another opinion would be helpful? I'm more than willing to volunteer my services."

"I'm not sure that's a good idea."

"Why not?"

"You'd be bored."

"Believe me, Annabella, going to Tulsa with you to shop would not be boring. I'd enjoy it."

"If you're certain you want to," she said hesitantly, then took a deep breath and said confidently, "We'll go in my car. Shall I pick you up at eight o'clock? That will get us to Tulsa by ten."

"That's very liberated of you," he said, grinning. "I'll be ready at eight."

"Don't blame me if you're bored."

"Not a chance. Are you ready to leave? We could go for an after-dinner stroll."

"A stroll? Even in Harmony it isn't a good idea to go walking after dark because . . . oh, you'd be with me, wouldn't you? I'm so accustomed to being alone and . . . yes, a walk sounds lovely."

"Annabella," Terry said, his voice low, "Remember that I'm here, won't you?"

For now, she thought. Temporarily. Now she could

add a walk in the moonlight with Terry to her store of memories.

The evening was pleasantly warm, and the moon was a silver globe in the heavens, with millions of stars twinkling their greetings.

With Annabella's hand clasped in his they started out, and Terry began telling her tales of growing up in Harmony. The sight of a certain house would evoke a memory of a prank or a party, and soon Annabella was laughing in delight at his stories.

She noticed how comfortable she was feeling, although she was acutely aware of the man by her side. She felt his heat, knew his strength, inhaled his special aroma.

Oh, how she wished he'd kiss her. She'd never been kissed in the moonlight.

They strolled through the small park, and Terry stopped, looking up at a huge oak tree they were standing next to.

"When I was eight years old," he said, smiling, "I kissed Patty Sue Mayfield under this tree, and she punched me right in the eye. I had a beaut of a shiner, and swore I'd never mess with older women again. Patty Sue was ten—much too old and mean for me!"

Annabella laughed.

Terry turned to face her, then slowly drew the yellow satin ribbon from her hair.

"So, tell me, Miss Annabella Abraham," he said. He combed his fingers through the wavy cascade, bringing some of the silken strands forward to sift through his fingers and float down over her breasts.

"If I were to kiss you under this big old oak tree here in the moonlight, would you punch me in the eye?"

"No," she said, her voice hushed.

"I truly am glad to hear it."

And Annabella was glad to know he was about to kiss her, she truly was.

And he truly did.

And it was glorious.

The kiss was long and powerful, sensuous and sweet. It was heat. Desire. Tongues meeting, bodies pressing close to feel, savor, taste, all that there was. Passion was rising, breathing becoming ragged, hearts beating wildly. The kiss was the promise of more, of what could be, should their hearts and minds whisper the message of consent. It was Annabella and Terry, with the silvery moon and stars and the ancient oak tree as witnesses.

"Oh, Annabella," Terry said, his voice gritty as he lifted his head, "That's all I can say, just 'Oh, Annabella,' because to tell you that I want you is something you already know."

"I—"

"Shh. Come on, I'll walk you home and kiss you good night at your door. This has been a special evening, Annabella."

"Yes. Yes, it has. Memories . . . memories are made from hours spent like this."

"I like the way that sounds."

"Terry, what time is it?"

He glanced at his watch, having no trouble seeing it in the silvery luminescence. "It's eleven thirty-two."

She smiled. "I can't remember when I've been up past ten o'clock."

Terry chuckled and circled her shoulders with his arm, tucking her close to his side.

"Changes, Miss Annabella," he said.

"You're absolutely right, Mr. Russell," she said. For now, just for now, she thought with a sudden wave of sadness. No, she wouldn't let herself feel sad. Nothing was going to spoil this evening, and tarnish these wondrous hours.

At the edge of the park Terry glanced back at the big oak tree.

"I must say, Annabella, that kissing you under that old tree was a helluva lot better than kissing Patty Sue Mayfield."

Annabella laughed in delight and Terry joined her.

A sudden breeze rippled the leaves of the oak tree, adding nature's music to the joyous sound of Annabella's and Terry's laughter.

Seven

The drive to Tulsa was pleasant, and as far as Annabella was concerned, the time was passing much too quickly. Terry offered to drive her car, so she settled into the passenger seat and simply enjoyed.

And there was, she soon realized, a great deal to enjoy. Terry was so close to her in the compact car, and she had a marvelous view of his broad shoulders and chest filling the open-neck, pale gray dress shirt he wore and of the muscles in his thighs beneath black slacks. She could examine his handsome profile to her heart's content and was the recipient of his flashing smile when he glanced over at her. She inhaled his spicy, male aroma, and watched his large hands as he maneuvered the car with relaxed expertise.

They talked on and on, moving from one topic to the next with an ease that amazed her. She'd never been comfortable taking part in casual conversation before, always feeling that no one would be particularly interested in what she had to say.

But not so with Terry, she mused. As far as she was concerned, they could keep driving forever, forget about shopping, just continue talking, sharing, getting to know each other in greater depth, with every passing mile.

When they reached Tulsa, Terry concentrated on the traffic, and Annabella indulged herself in a private rerun of the previous night. Terry had kissed her good night at her door as he'd said he would, and afterward the desire radiating from the blue depths of Terry's eyes had caused her knees to tremble and her heart to race. She'd mumbled her good night and gone quickly inside the house.

What would have happened, she wondered, if she'd invited Terry in? She wanted to make love with him. That fact no longer shocked her, it was simply there, true and honest. But, oh heavens, she knew nothing about pleasing a man, had no experience in being all that she should be as a woman. Terry was worldly, social, moving in circles that included jet-setters and captains of industry. He'd no doubt been with women who knew exactly what to do and say.

She was, Annabella thought glumly, just a naive librarian from Harmony, Oklahoma, who now indulged in romantic fantasy about making love. Terry Russell was out of her league, out of her—no, now wait a minute. That was the old Annabella talking, the drab, fade-into-a-corner Annabella. The Annabella Abraham sitting in this car was making changes. She wouldn't allow herself to fall victim to her own self-doubts, her shyness, her quiet acceptance of the way things were.

This was *her* turn, she thought firmly. For these stolen days and precious hours she was Cinderella, transforming herself into all she wished to be. And beside her was the handsomest, dearest, most magnificent prince on the face of the earth. While he was with her, she had the courage to make whatever changes suited her.

"There's a shopping mall," Terry said, bringing Annabella back from her reverie. "We ought to be able to find what you need in there."

"Yes, all right," Annabella said, smoothing the material of her skirt.

Terry glanced over at her, then eased into the next lane. It had been a nice drive, he thought. Annabella was fun to talk to—quick, intelligent, knowledgeable about a multitude of subjects. He'd allowed her voice to float over him like a velvet cloak, making him infinitely glad that she was with him.

He couldn't remember when he'd found it so enjoyable to really talk to a woman, he realized. Annabella wasn't coy or flirtatious; she was real and honest. He felt as though he'd known her all his life. He sensed that he could tell her his innermost thoughts if he chose and she would listen, *and hear*, what he had to say. She was really something.

Terry parked the car, then came around to open Annabella's door and assist her out of the vehicle. He'd made no comment on the drab brown dress she wore, realizing that the yellow sundress was no doubt the only surprise she had in her closet. Her hair was once more in the bun at the nape of her neck, and she wore sturdy brown shoes.

The little brown sparrow, he thought, as they walked across the parking lot. But not really. The Annabella he knew was there beneath the frumpy exterior, and he had a sudden urge to haul her into his arms and kiss her, taste her, feel her breasts crushed to his chest.

He knew he could have made love to her last night. After the discussions they'd had at dinner on the subject, then the kiss under the big oak tree, there was no doubt in his mind that Annabella could have been his.

But he'd known that the time wasn't right. It was too soon, too fast, for her. And strangely enough, he'd realized it was too soon for him too. Something new and different was happening to him. When he and Annabella made love, it was going to be perfect for both of them.

They entered the mall and wandered over to a fountain that had pennies shimmering in the bottom.

"Want to make a wish?" Terry said.

"No," Annabella said, smiling.

"Why not?"

"I don't think I'd have any idea what to wish for. I haven't had the usual training course in making wishes. I never had a birthday cake with candles to wish on."

Terry frowned. "You never had a birthday cake?"

"No. Terry, look at all those stores. I don't know where to begin."

"Easy to do," he said, taking her hand. "We walk into the first one we come to and see what they have. You need dresses, blouses, skirts, tops, shoes, and a pair of jeans."

"Jeans?"

"No one should go through life without jeans, Annabella. It's un-American."

"Oh, dear. I just don't—"

"No backing out now. Come on."

Terry took charge.

There were so many clothes to see and select from that they all seemed to mesh together in a swirl of bright colors. Feeling about four years old, but not caring, Annabella stood quietly as Terry went through the racks. He pulled a dress out, held it at arm's length, shook his head, and put it back. The next one received his approval, and he handed a red-and-white-striped dress to Annabella.

"It looks like a barber pole," she said.

"It's classy. Don't judge it until you've tried it on. Ah, here is another."

"Blue and green flowers? Terry, people will see me coming a mile away."

"Trust me."

Annabella rolled her eyes and draped the flowered dress over her arm on top of the red-and-white-striped one.

And on it went.

Terry finally pointed her in the direction of the fitting room and said he wanted to see her in each creation. The red and white barber pole looked like a red and white barber pole when she put it on, and Terry gave it a thumbs down. But the blue-and-green-flowered dress was extremely attractive, and

Annabella peered at her reflection in amazement. Terry gave it a thumbs up.

They went from store to store, and the pile of packages Terry held grew bigger. There was a silky, teal blue dress that hugged Annabella in all the right places. A raspberry-colored blouse with a burgundy skirt. Jeans and a bright yellow sweater. There was a black-and-white-striped number that Annabella was certain would transform her into a zebra, but it was stunning and very sophisticated. There was a dress of burnt orange, and another in a lovely shade of lavender.

"It reminds me of violets," Annabella said.

"Knew you'd love it. Next!"

"Terry, I'm getting tired."

"No time for tired. We have a mission to complete here. We'll have a quick lunch, then start on shoes."

"How about a long, leisurely lunch, then we go home?"

"No."

"Didn't think so," she said with a sigh. "I've taken off my clothes more times than a stripper."

Terry hooted with laughter.

All through the afternoon, Annabella tried on dozens of pairs of shoes and foggily waited for Terry to accept or reject the selections. She also bought a pair of white slacks and a kelly green blouse, which she wore out of a store with white sandals on her feet. When she complained of a headache, Terry deftly removed the pins from her hair, letting it swing freely down her back.

"That's much better," Annabella said.

"Good. There's a store over there we haven't checked out yet. Let's go."

"I don't want to."

"Tough."

"Were you ever a marine sergeant?" Annabella asked, glaring at him.

"Annabella, this is fun."

"It is?"

He smiled warmly at her. "It's important, Annabella, you know that, don't you? You deserve pretty things like these, deserve to be all you can be. You look so beautiful in everything that's in these packages. You've liked how you've looked, haven't you?"

She smiled. "Yes. Yes, I have. I can't quite believe it's me when I look in the mirror. There shouldn't be so much importance put on outward appearance, but I must admit I'm enjoying feeling pretty and feminine. I'm sorry to be so crabby. You've been wonderful. I never dreamed I'd own clothes like these."

"Changes, Annabella. That's what this is all about. Come on. One more store, then we'll have dinner before we drive back."

"Yes, all right," she said. She glanced over at the packages in Terry's arms, knowing there were twice as many already in the trunk of the car.

Such lovely clothes. She wondered if she would wear them after Terry left Harmony. She'd said she enjoyed feeling pretty and feminine, but that's because Terry had told her she looked wonderful. The image in the mirror was a stranger, someone she didn't know, and it took Terry's approval to make the metamorphosis acceptable. It was all becoming terribly confusing, but she was so tired, she couldn't begin to sort things through.

It was dark by the time Terry pulled into the driveway at his parents' house.

"Would you like me to get my dad's car and follow you home?" he said. "You're really beat."

"Oh, no, I'm fine."

"Are you sure?"

"Yes, really. Terry, thank you for today. I know I would have come home empty-handed if it weren't for you."

"I enjoyed it and I definitely wasn't bored." He shifted slightly in the seat to face her. "Annabella, I want to say something. Earlier today you said that there shouldn't be so much importance placed on outward appearance. I tend to agree with you, but only to a point. How we dress has a lot to do with how we feel about ourselves. We're creating an image that affects the way we act, our self-confidence, the whole nine yards."

Annabella nodded, but didn't comment.

"I just want you to know that whether you were decked out in something we bought today, or in a flour sack, I'd still know who you are, Annabella. I feel as if I've known you for a lifetime and I like that. I like that very, very much. The clothes you bought today are a gift to yourself, something you deserve to have. I enjoy seeing you look so beautiful, but if you decided to throw all that stuff out the window, it would be okay too. Understand?"

"Yes," she whispered.

"Whatever you do, do it for yourself."

No! No, he didn't understand, Annabella thought frantically. The changes weren't for her, they were for him, for the time they would have together. And now he was saying the clothes didn't matter to him? They were for her? Only for her? She didn't want the clothes, didn't know who she was when she was wearing them. Do it for herself? She didn't know how!

"Annabella?"

"Yes, I hear you. I realize I'm being very quiet, but I'm awfully tired."

"I'm sure you are. It's been a big day. I'll see you tomorrow." He slipped his hand to the nape of her neck, then leaned forward to claim her mouth in a deep, searing kiss that left Annabella trembling and wanting more. "Sleep well, Annabella. Good night."

"Good night," she said softly.

As Annabella drove home voices of confusion shouted in her mind. She forced herself not to listen. She was so very weary and wished only to crawl into bed and sleep. Tears misted her eyes and she blinked them angrily away, not even knowing why, on top of everything else, she felt like having a long cry.

By the time she'd toted all the packages into the house, carefully hung her purchases in the closet, and had a warm bath, she was nearly numb with fatigue. She slipped into bed, closed her eyes, and was asleep within minutes.

Terry found his parents on the screened porch.

"So, you had quite a day of shopping," Mary said. "I didn't know you enjoyed that sort of thing."

"I didn't either," Terry said, settling into the swing. "I've never been shopping for clothes with a woman before. Misty never asked me to go with her, and it never occurred to me to tag along. Today was a first."

"And?" Mary asked.

"It was great," Terry said, nodding. "I got so I could tell at a glance what would look good on Annabella. After I screwed up with a red-and-white-striped dress, I started getting the knack of it. She got so many terrific things. She looked sensational in the clothes. Tonight she was so worn out, she could hardly move. I really put her through her paces."

"Why?" Mike asked.

Terry looked at him in surprise. "What?"

"Why did you insist that Miss Annabella have a new, up-to-date wardrobe?"

"I didn't insist. You're misunderstanding the situation, Dad. I did for Annabella what you did for me. I pointed out to her that perhaps it was time for her to take a good long look at her life and see if it was the way she really wanted it to be."

Mike tapped his pipe on the rim of the ashtray. "I see. Well, I had that conversation with you because I love you. What were your motives behind bringing it up to Miss Annabella?"

"Well, I . . . I care about her. I just pointed out that she could have more in her life if she wanted it. The shopping trip was her idea, so you can see that she's decided to make some changes."

"But why?" Mike asked again. "That question is still there."

"For herself."

"Are you sure of that, Terry?" Mike asked. "What if these changes she's making are for you? Miss Annabella might end up getting hurt, and I'd hate to see that happen."

"Hurt? By me? Dad, I have no intention of hurting her."

"Sometimes," Mary said softly, "it can't be helped."

"I care about Annabella Abraham, understand?" Terry said, getting to his feet. "I care a whole helluva lot, and I don't intend to let her get hurt. I really don't give a damn what she's wearing when I take her in my arms and . . ." His voice trailed off. "Forget it. Just forget the whole thing."

"Yes, dear," Mary said sweetly.

"Your turn, Dad," Terry said gruffly. "Add your next two cents worth."

"Nope," Mike said, lacing his hands across his chest and smiling contentedly. "I found out what I needed to know."

"Which is?" Terry said.

Mike just kept on smiling.

"That's it. I'm going to bed," Terry said. "How did I turn out to be such a well-adjusted, normal guy, when I have such wacko parents?"

"Oh, land's sake," Mary said, "that's the funniest thing I've ever heard." She dissolved in a fit of laughter.

"Good night, Mr. and Mrs. Russell," Terry said stiffly, then stalked into the house.

The sound of his parents' delighted laughter followed him down the hall.

•   •   •

At two A.M. Terry gave up his futile attempt to sleep. He'd done nothing but toss and turn and get himself totally tangled in the sheets. He left the bed, pulled on a pair of jeans, and went downstairs to the screened porch, where he paced back and forth for several minutes before collapsing onto the swing.

He replayed in his mind yet again the events of the day spent with Annabella, then heard his father's words echoing in his mind. He also heard his own heated declaration that he had no intention of hurting Annabella because he cared for her.

He did care for her.

But there in the dark of night, alone, Terry knew that his feelings went deeper than that.

"Damn," he said, drawing a shuddering breath.

He was in love with Miss Annabella Abraham.

He should have known, Terry thought. He should have realized the very moment he first saw her at the airfield that his life was about to undergo a major change.

Terry smiled and laced his hands behind his head, sliding lower in the swing. It had happened step by step, he realized, prompted by his loving father's urging to look inside himself to see if he was happy. And little by little, smile by smile, kiss by kiss, Annabella was filling him to overflowing, making him whole again.

And he loved her.

"I'll be damned," Terry said, still smiling. It felt good. Annabella was the woman he wanted to spend the rest of his life with. He could see her by his side, growing big with his child, being his partner, his other half, for the remainder of their days. Annabella.

But then his smile faded as he remembered his father's words of warning that the changes Annabella was making might be for Terry rather than for herself. Sure, he liked her looking sensational, any man would. But if to be happy, and to be herself, Annabella had to stay as the little sparrow, so be it. He knew who she really was, so warm, giving, passionate. She was intelligent, and fun, and they shared everything. The outer wrappings didn't matter.

Terry sat up, his thoughts racing. What had he done? Had Annabella bought all those clothes for him? Was she trying to be what she felt he wanted her to be? Did her depth of caring for him go so deep that she was willing to lose her own identity to please him? That was wrong.

But how, he wondered frantically, was he to know what she was really thinking? Was it clear to her why she was making the changes, or was she totally confused? Were the changes for him, or for herself?

Damn, so many questions, he thought, and the answers were so important. Their future was at stake. What now? What did he do next? Ah, hell, now *he* was so confused he couldn't think straight.

A slight sound behind him caused Terry to turn, and he saw the shadow of his father standing in the doorway to the porch.

"I thought you might be out here," Mike said quietly.

"Couldn't sleep."

"I only said what needed saying."

"I know that, Dad. I hope I'm as wise as you are someday, but I doubt I will be."

"Wisdom comes in time. It comes with years of loving and being loved. Have you figured it out yet?"

Terry took a deep breath and let it out slowly. "I love her. I love her, Dad. I'm in love with Annabella."

Mike nodded. "I know. I just wondered if you knew it." He walked across the porch and stared out at the star-studded sky. "How do you feel about it?"

"Confused, at the moment," Terry said. "A part of me wants to shout it from the rooftops, go wake up Annabella and tell her, start making plans and . . . but then come the doubts. Dad, what if you're right? What if Annabella is making changes in her life for me instead of for herself? Hey, it would be great that her feelings for me run that deeply already, but the overall picture is wrong. She has to be true to herself, who she really is, first."

Mike chuckled softly. "I told you that wisdom comes with loving. You're a wise man, Terry." He turned to look at him. "I've heard what I needed to know. I'll head on back to bed now."

"Hey, wait. Aren't you going to help me out here?"

"Nope. You've got your head on straight. You'll do what's right."

"I'm glad you think so. I don't have the foggiest idea what to do. There are so many questions that have to have answers."

"Take it slow and easy. Watch, listen, pay attention, that's all I can tell you." He paused. "You know, you discovered that you love Annabella by listening to your heart. There are a lot more answers there than you realize."

"I hope so."

"I know so. Good night."

"Good night, Dad, and thanks. Thank you more than I can say."

"You're welcome, Terry. You'll have a son or daughter someday, and you'll pass on the wisdom to another generation." He started toward the door.

"Dad?" Terry said quietly.

Mike stopped. "Yes?"

"I love you."

Mike was quiet for a long moment, and his voice was thick with emotion when he spoke. "I love you, too, my son. By happy, Terry." He went into the house.

"Be happy," Terry repeated to the night. "Dear God, I hope so. Ah, Annabella Abraham, can I make you happy? Do you love me, Annabella?"

With a weary shake of his head Terry got slowly to his feet and went into the house.

The next morning Annabella stood in front of her closet, feeling as overwhelmed as she had in the shopping mall.

All those fantastic clothes and she didn't know what to wear. It was as though, she realized, they belonged to someone else and had been placed in her closet by mistake. The large dip in her checkbook balance would verify that the clothes were hers, but they looked so out of place there in her bedroom.

Annabella sat down on the edge of the bed. This was absurd, she told herself. Those lovely things were hers, and all she had to do was decide what to wear. Heavens, it had been so much easier when Terry had been with her, urging her on, telling her she looked beautiful in the bright creations.

But now, in the light of the new day, sitting there alone in her bedroom, she felt like a little girl about to play dress-up, about to pretend for awhile to be someone she wasn't.

But that, she thought dismally, was exactly how it was. It was all make-believe, and temporary. Terry included. She knew that, but for some reason this morning, the scenario was terribly sad and terribly depressing.

She threw up her hands and went to the closet, reaching for the dress with the blue and green flowers. She put it on, fixed her hair with a blue grosgrain ribbon, then started to leave the bedroom.

Suddenly she stopped as she caught a reflection of herself in the full-length mirror.

She blinked, turned slowly, and scrutinized herself from head to toe.

"Oh, Annabella," she said, awe evident in her voice, "you look . . . you look lovely."

She'd seen herself in the dress in the store but that was yesterday when she was Cinderella, and Terry, the prince, was there to reassure her she was attractive. How strange it felt to have the dress on, here, alone, and be registering the same reactions. She looked lovely! And, yes, she felt feminine, and, oh, so very pretty, and—

"Have some tea, Annabella," she said sternly, "and just calm yourself down."

She swished out of the bedroom. She swished because the skirt of the dress was full and felt marvelous swinging around her legs. She was certainly making a hoopla out of a dress, and Terry wasn't even there to see it.

She glanced at her watch, carried her cup of spiced-apple tea into the living room, then settled into the rocker. She did some of her best thinking in that rocker, she decided, and some thinking was overdue.

Terry.

Well, she thought dryly, there was no doubt as to where her mind was centered. Wonderful, warm, magnificent Terry. Terry, who had told her after returning from Tulsa to make the changes for herself, to wear the new clothes for herself or toss them out the window, whichever suited her.

But the changes, the clothes, were for him, her mind taunted.

Really? a little voice questioned. Then why had she swished out of the bedroom? Why was she just tickled to pieces over the way she looked and how she felt in her pretty, pretty dress? Wasn't that rather strange, and a bit conceited, to announce to oneself that one looked stunning, and feminine, and border-line beautiful? It certainly sounded conceited to her. Good grief, this was confusing. Yesterday, in the stores, she hadn't felt pretty until Terry told her she was. But now? What was happening here?

"I have no idea," she said, getting to her feet. "Go to work, Annabella."

At the library Mrs. Perdy's eyes widened when she saw Annabella. "Miss Annabella, that is a splendid dress, just splendid," she gushed. "Land's sake, it just outshines that yellow sundress you wore the other day. Mercy me, I can't get over the change in you. Of course, now I know for certain there's a man behind it all. He is handsome, that Terry. He was a little devil as a youngster, but he's grown up just fine. Mighty fine. I think it's marvelous how you're fixing yourself up so special for Terry."

Annabella frowned. "Well," she said slowly, "that's not entirely true because . . . because I wore the dress here to the library. If," she went on, thinking as she spoke, "if I were wearing it just for Terry, why didn't I wait until I was going to be with him?"

Mrs. Perdy pressed a chubby finger to one of her chins. "I don't know," she said, matching Annabella's frown. "Why did you wear the dress to work? Of course, Terry did show up here the other day."

"Yes, but I don't know for sure that he's going to come today. This is confusing."

"Well, maybe not," Mrs. Perdy said. "Seems to me, Miss Annabella, that you're long past due being the woman you could be. You're just a late bloomer, honey, that's all. I'm not saying that Terry Russell didn't nudge you along a bit, but I'd guess you're wearing that dress today because you want to look so splendid for yourself. If Terry happens by, then lucky for him."

"Oh, Mrs. Perdy, I don't think that could be true. That's disturbing. I'm not one to draw attention to myself, but that's exactly what I'm doing. I wore the yellow sundress, then, today . . . why am I doing this? The changes, the clothes, they're supposed to be for . . . and it's all temporary because . . . but here I stand in blue and green flowers and . . . oh, mercy."

"Now you're confusing me, Miss Annabella," Mrs. Perdy said. "I didn't understand all of that."

"That's all right, I didn't either," Annabella said with a sigh.

"Here comes Ralph Newberry," Mrs. Perdy whispered. "I swear that man costs this library a fortune in tissues. You'd think he'd bring a box of his own with a nose like that."

"Good morning, Mrs. Perdy," Ralph Newberry said. "Good morning, Miss . . ." His gaze swept over Annabella. "Is that you, Miss Annabella? I must say you look . . . you look . . ."

"Pretty as a picture," Mrs. Perdy prompted.

"Yes, indeed," Ralph said. "I noticed that yellow dress you wore too." He sighed dramatically, then reached in his pocket for a tissue to dab at his nose. "I guess it's true, then." He sighed again.

"What's true?" Annabella said.

"That you're stepping out with Terry Russell," Ralph said. "I saw him in here myself the other day and did hear tell at the café that you spent the entire day in Tulsa with him. A man with severe allergies can't compete with the likes of Terry. I was so hoping, Miss Annabella, that the rumors weren't fact, but seeing you in that dress tells me you're all gussied up for Terry. He's a lucky man."

Annabella narrowed her eyes and planted her hands on her hips. "You just hold it right there, Ralph Newberry. Do you see Terry Russell in this library? No, you do not. Do you see me in this dress? Yes, you do. And do you know why? I wore it for me! *Me*,

Mr. Newberry, because I'm important, I'm a woman, and I think I look . . . gorgeous!"

"Hear, hear," Mrs. Perdy said, beaming.

"There's no call to holler, Miss Annabella," Ralph said. "I've never known you to raise your voice as you've been doing lately. I hear what you're saying, but what's the point in getting all gussied up if it isn't for a man? Doesn't make any sense to me at all."

Annabella shrieked. Ralph clutched his tissue with both hands and took a hasty step backward, his eyes wide. "Ralph Newberry, go—go blow your nose!"

And with that, Miss Annabella Abraham spun around, stomped into her office, and slammed the door.

Eight

To Annabella the day seemed endless. Mrs. Perdy left early, with a soft smile for Annabella and a pat on her hand, nearly causing Annabella to fling herself into the large woman's arms and weep.

She was so close to tears, it was ridiculous, and Annabella had no idea what circumstances might set her off on a loud crying jag. She was a befuddled, confused mess, and while she realized that tears weren't going to solve a thing, she also knew that once they were started—it was going to be difficult to stop them.

She did her work feeling like a robot, checking books in, out, placing them on the shelves. Everyone who came into the library complimented her on her pretty dress, and before long her smile felt like a plastic mask, her "thank-yous" forced and hollow.

Ralph Newberry skittered out the door like a scared rabbit, and Annabella didn't blame him, considering she'd screamed at him like a deranged banshee. Such undignified behavior for a librarian, and so unladylike. On top of everything else she now owed Ralph Newberry a sincere apology. On top of everything else, Annabella thought wearily as she replaced books on the shelves. *What* everything else? She had to start sorting through the jumble in her mind before she went totally insane.

She glanced down at her dress, seeing the bright, pretty flowers on the soft material. It had all been so clear, she mused dismally. The changes. The changes, the clothes, her hairdo, her responses were all to have been for Terry. For awhile. Stolen days, hours, minutes. Temporary.

But there she'd stood, stating—no, yelling—to the entire library that she'd worn the dress for herself, the woman, the person she was.

But who was she?

Annabella stopped statue-still in the quiet library and looked around, seeing that for the moment she was alone. The question came again, louder this time, beating against her brain.

Who was she?

Who was Miss Annabella Abraham?

Her trembling legs refused to hold her, and she sat down on a chair at one of the tables. She'd always known who she was. She'd learned to expect nothing and was therefore not disappointed when the days faded one into the next with no surprises or deviation. Her life had been quiet, organized, predictable. She'd never questioned it, or her happiness, and considered herself to be content.

And then . . .

Terry Russell.

From the minute Terry had zoomed out of the heavens in that terrifying plane she'd won, her life had been turned upside down and inside out.

Because of Terry she now knew she was a woman with desires, needs, and wants. She gloried in her own femininity and in her ability to respond to the kisses and touches of the most magnificent man she'd ever met. A man who made her feel alive and real, and who could make her body hum with passion. A man who said she was beautiful and special and rare, and who could melt her bones with one dazzling smile.

Terry.

The only man she'd ever wanted to make love with.

Terry Russell.

The only man she had ever loved.

Annabella stiffened in her chair. "What?" she whispered. What? Oh, no. Please no, it couldn't have happened, it couldn't be true. She wasn't in love with Terry.

Yes, she was.

"Annabella," she said, a sad tone to her voice, "what a foolish thing you've gone and done."

She pressed her fingertips to her throbbing temples and willed herself not to cry. Her confusion, she knew, was worse than she'd thought. She was in love. *But who was she?* Who had fallen in love with Terry? Annabella Abraham, librarian, of Harmony, Oklahoma? Quiet, drab, sedate Annabella? Or the Annabella who had emerged, blossomed, under Terry's knowing touch? The temporary Annabella, the one she allowed to step forward for as long as Terry was in her life?

She was in love with Terry Russell, but she didn't know, really know, who this woman was who loved him.

It was as though, she realized, there were two of her: the old Annabella, the new Annabella; the permanent, the temporary. The only thing she suddenly knew for certain was that her love for Terry encompassed both of the Annabella Abrahams. The love was real, true, honest. What she didn't know was which one of the Annabellas was real.

Because she no longer knew who she really was.

With a sigh Annabella got to her feet and glanced at the clock. It was time to go home. Home to her little house on Peach Street, her haven, her quiet place. But now, as she pictured it in her mind, it was too quiet, too empty, too lonely—without Terry.

Annabella closed up the library, then got into her car and drove slowly through town. She glanced around, as though seeing Harmony for the first time, examining it through the eyes of a stranger. She felt removed from herself, detached, viewing what she saw as one might do if one were considering moving there. It was a quiet small town, offering little to its residents in the way of entertainment or excitement, yet it was peaceful and pretty. It was a town that would welcome a shy librarian who wished to live simply, belong to the Quilting Club, and make homemade bread and sugar tea-cookies for the church bake sales.

Harmony, Oklahoma, had suited her just fine—before Terry.

Annabella pulled into her driveway, turned off the ignition, and got out of the car, very aware that her headache was no better. She walked across the small lawn, then gasped and stopped as a tall figure leveled himself up from her front steps.

"Hello, Annabella," Terry said quietly. There she was, he thought, the woman he loved, beautiful Annabella. He wanted to take her into his arms, declare his love, and never ever let her go.

"Hello, Terry," she said softly, telling her feet to move her forward. She loved this man. Oh, dear heaven, how she loved him. In the midst of all her confusion that fact was so clear, so warming, so wonderful. She wouldn't think about anything else at the moment except that she deeply loved Terry Russell.

She crossed the lawn and stood in front of him, drinking in the very sight of him as she looked up into his blue eyes.

"I brought you these," he said.

Annabella blinked, then looked down. There, in Terry's big, strong, tanned hand, was a delicate bouquet of violets.

To Annabella those dainty flowers being offered to her by this man were the most precious, most thoughtful, most meaningful gift she had ever received. She was overwhelmed with emotion. It was too much to deal with on a day that had drained her, left her exhausted and vulnerable. It was her final undoing.

And she burst into tears.

Terry's eyes widened in shock. He stared at Annabella, at the violets, then back at Annabella. "Annabella, what—I—" he asked. "What's wrong?"

Annabella covered her face with her hands and shook her head.

"Let's go into the house," he said. "Come on, Annabella."

With tears streaming down her face Annabella managed to unlock the door and go inside, with Terry close at her heels. She sank into the sofa, leaned her head back, and closed her eyes, making no attempt to stop crying. Terry put the violets on the end table, sat down next to her, then carefully, slowly, as if she might shatter into pieces, held her to him and cradled her head on his shoulder. Annabella wept. She clutched his shirt in tight fists and cried.

Terry didn't know what to do, or say, or what was wrong with her, so he just held her. The sound of her sad sobs tore at his heart, which pounded like a wild drum in his chest.

At last she quieted, and Terry reached in his back pocket for a handkerchief, which he gave to her as she straightened and drew a wobbly breath.

"I'm sorry," she said, her voice trembling as she wiped away the tears.

"What's wrong? Annabella, please, talk to me."

She clutched her hands tightly in her lap and stared at them, unable to look at him.

"Nothing," she said. "Everything. I don't know."

"Is it the gossip about us? The whole town is buzzing, but that's how it is in a small town, you know that. People are bored here, ready for any news to liven things up. I purposely didn't come to the library today because they were all watching for me to do it. Is that why you're upset? The gossip?"

"No."

"Could you look at me?"

"No."

"It's a little tough to carry on a serious conversation with your ear, Annabella. Please look at me."

"No."

"Okay," he said slowly. "We'll do this your way. You're not upset about the gossip. Check. The violets. You saw the violets and fell apart. You've suddenly decided that you hate violets?"

Annabella's head popped up and she looked at Terry. "Oh, no, no. I love violets. That bouquet is so pretty, and you were so sweet to bring them, and I didn't even say thank you, which was rude, and . . . oh-h-h." And the tears started again.

"Annabella, don't cry. I can't handle this. You've got to tell me what's wrong so I can fix it."

She sniffled. "Fix it?"

"Well, yes. We'll work it out together, whatever it is, but I have to know what we're dealing with here. You've got to tell me so we can figure out what to do."

"Why?"

"Why what?" he said, obviously confused.

"I'm the one who's crying. I'm the one who's upset. Why would you be concerned about fixing it, solving my problems? They are, after all, my problems."

He gripped her shoulders and turned her toward him. "Because that's how it's done. Your sadness is my sadness, your joy is my joy. Right now you're sad, so together we're going to make you unsad." He frowned. "I don't think that's a word. Annabella, you're not alone, don't you see? I'm here, we're together."

"For now," she said, her bottom lip quivering.

"For now? Oh, you mean because I'm home on vacation. Well, we need to talk about that, about a lot of things in fact. But first up is to have you tell me what's wrong."

"It's too complicated, too confusing, Terry. It doesn't make sense to me, so how could I explain it to you?"

"Try. Just jump in and say something, and we'll take it from there."

"I . . . I don't know who I am," she said, her eyes brimming with fresh tears.

Terry opened his mouth, closed it, then shook his head slightly. "Could you run that by me again?"

"See? I told you it wouldn't make sense. There's no point in discussing this." She attempted to pull out of his grasp.

"Whoa," he said. "Problems don't get solved by ignoring them or running away. We've got to talk it all through. So, okay, you don't know who you are. That's a heavy-duty statement, Annabella. Could you expand on that for me?"

"This dress," she said, her voice raising. "Why did I wear this dress today?"

He grinned at her. "Because you'd be arrested if you went to the library naked?"

"That does it," she said. She wiggled out of his grasp, got to her feet, and marched toward the kitchen. "I'm hungry, my head hurts, I need a cup of tea, and I don't wish to discuss any of this further with you, Mr. Russell."

"Hey!" Terry said, jumping to his feet. He caught up with her in the kitchen. "I was just trying to lighten things up a little. I hate to see you so sad,

Annabella. I want to help, but I can't if you won't let me."

Annabella ran water into the teakettle and set it on the stove. "It's my problem. Would you like to stay for dinner?"

"Sure, I'll stay if it's no trouble." He paused. "It's our problem because it's making you unhappy. You said you don't know who you are. What exactly does that mean?"

She took two steaks out of the freezer. "That I'm confused regarding some of my actions, the reasons why I'm doing certain things."

Ah, damn, Terry thought, the changes. Now the reference to the dress made sense. Why was she wearing the pretty dress? It could very well be that she didn't know if it was for him or for her. He'd pushed her too hard. Now she was upset, sad, and crying, for heaven's sake. He had to fix this. Somehow.

Terry watched as Annabella defrosted the steaks in a small microwave, then placed them on the broiler in the oven. Next she took the makings for a salad from the refrigerator.

"Salad," he said. "I can make a salad. I'm a great salad maker. I'll have you know that I'm famous for my salads."

"So, make the salad," Annabella said. "I'm going to go take some aspirin. There's a bowl above the plates in the cupboard."

"Right," Terry said. Terrific, he thought. He'd never made a salad in his life. Well, how tough could it be? Chop up the lettuce, put it in the bowl. Nothing to it. The important thing was to keep Annabella talking, communicating, to not allow her to retreat inside herself and leave him alone. And lonely. He loved her and needed to share with her.

Annabella returned to the kitchen and turned the steaks over in the broiler. She peered around Terry and into the bowl.

"What is that?" she said.

"My salad. Don't you recognize a salad when you see one?"

"Yes, I do, when I see one. What I see there is chunks . Four big chunks of lettuce, four big chunks of tomato, four big chunks of—"

"I know what's in my salad, Annabella," Terry said indignantly. "You don't have to give me an inventory. This is what is known as a . . ."

"Chunky salad."

"Correct. This recipe has been handed down in the Russell family for generations."

"Bull."

Terry gasped, covered his heart with his hand, and leaned back against the wall.

" 'Bull?' " he said, in mock horror. "You opened that luscious mouth of yours, and said 'Bull'? Madam, please, my sensibilities are being offended here."

Annabella laughed.

She laughed because she was so tired of crying and because Terry was trying so hard to bring her out of her gloomy mood. She laughed because he had just made the worst salad she'd ever seen, but it had been such a sweet gesture on his part. She laughed because it kept her from thinking, and she was just too confused to think.

"Ah, now, that is the music of angels," Terry said, still leaning against the wall. He held out his hand to her. "Come here, Annabella. Come here and let me kiss you hello, because I never did get a chance to do that. Come here, come here, come here."

And she went.

She went to have his arms tighten around her and his mouth claim hers. She went to press her body to his and savor the sensations of desire that rocketed through her. She went to the man she loved.

Terry's hands roamed over her back as the kiss intensified. He spread his legs slightly and nestled her to him as his hands went lower, over the slope of her buttocks. The material of the dress was little barrier between his hands and Annabella's soft curves. He could feel himself reaching a point of no return.

"Annabella," he said, his voice raspy, "the steaks."

"What?"

"Burning."

"That's nice. Oh!" She spun around and yanked open the broiler. "The steaks aren't burning, they look just right."

"Well, they would have been burning," he said. *He* was burning. Wasn't that enough? "Can't have burnt steaks to go with this outstanding salad."

Annabella laughed and put the steaks on a plate. As she turned she found Terry staring at her, desire still evident in his smoky blue eyes. Her own body was thrumming with heat, with want. Their gazes held, sending the message, receiving it.

"We'd better—" Terry started, then cleared his throat roughly, "eat while the steaks are hot."

"Hot," Annabella repeated absently, unable to tear her gaze from his.

"Bad word choice," he said, then picked up the bowl of salad.

As they ate, Annabella forgot about her long, miserable day. Beneath the relaxed atmosphere at the table a current of sexual tension was building, crackling, becoming nearly palpable in its intensity.

After dinner they moved into the living room.

"Would you like some blackberry brandy?" Annabella asked. She arranged the violets in a small vase, purposely avoiding looking at Terry. "I found the brandy in a cupboard. It apparently belonged to my Aunt Bessie."

"Yes, if you're having some."

"Well, I've never tasted it but . . . yes, I'll give it a try."

Annabella poured the brandy into small crystal glasses, then joined Terry on the sofa. Darkness was inching its way across the room, and after handing him his glass, she turned on the lamp on the end table. She met his gaze and he lifted his glass.

"A toast," he said. "Here's to you, Miss Annabella Abraham."

"Thank you," she said, then took a swallow of the brandy. It was syrupy sweet and warmed Annabella all the way to her toes. She blinked. "Goodness."

"Potent stuff," Terry said, smiling. But then he set his glass on the table, and his smile was gone when he looked at her again. "Annabella, I want to kiss you, now, right this minute, but I'm going to be very honest with you. If I take you in my arms, I'm not going to want to let you go. I want you. I want to make love to you. So, I'm not going to kiss you. We'll talk, or play gin rummy, or whatever."

"I—"

"But, Annabella, there's something you have to know. I'll say it, then we'll still play gin rummy, but—Annabella, I love you. That's as clear as I can make it. No flowery speeches, just the truth. I love you, Annabella Abraham, I truly do."

For a moment Annabella thought that Terry was speaking to someone else and that she should look over her shoulder to see who had come into the room. A funny buzzing noise rang in her ears, then disappeared, along with the room. All she saw was Terry, and the warmth, the tenderness, and the raw desire in his eyes.

He loved her, her heart sang.

Dear heaven, how could this be true? Terry Russell loved her. Her? Annabella Abraham?

Which Annabella? a nagging little voice questioned. The old or the new? The one she'd changed into or . . .

No, no, it didn't matter, her heart whispered. Not now. Nothing mattered but the glorious fact that he loved her as she loved him.

Should she tell him of her love? she wondered. If she did, she'd have to qualify it. She'd have to say, "I love you, too, Terry. My love is real, but I'm not sure which Annabella is real." No, no, she didn't want to spoil this moment. Nothing must spoil this moment. This was a turning point in her life. Terry Russell loved her.

She set her glass on the end table. "I . . . I don't know how to play gin rummy," she said, hardly above a whisper. "You love me?"

"I do."

"Oh, Terry, please, kiss me, hold me."

"Annabella, no. Don't you understand? I just can't handle having to let you go, not tonight."

"I do understand. You want to make love to me, and that's what I want, too."

"Annabella . . ."

"You know I have no experience. You know I don't have any idea how to please you, but I do want you. That's as honest as I can be, too, Terry."

"Are you sure?"

"I won't regret my actions, I promise you that. Terry, please, kiss me before I shatter into a million pieces."

With a groan he gathered her into his arms, his mouth claiming hers, his tongue meeting hers. Annabella circled his neck with her arms and leaned into him. The kiss was urgent, hungry, tasting of blackberry brandy. It was a kiss of no return, no turning back, as heated passion ran rampant within them.

He loved her, Terry thought hazily, and now she would be his. But what about her earlier tears, her statement that she didn't know who she was? No, he couldn't think about any of that now. This was their night.

Terry lifted his head and cradled her face in his hands. "Are you frightened, Annabella?"

"Of you? No. Of not pleasing you? Yes."

"Oh, don't even think that. You please me just by walking into the room, by being yourself. This isn't a test you have to pass. We will be sharing the most beautiful, intimate act that a man and woman can share. Come into the bedroom with me, Annabella."

"Yes," she whispered.

The glow from the living room lamp cast a rosy hue over the bedroom. Terry smiled when he saw the violet-covered bedspread, then threw it back to reveal crisp white sheets. He turned to find Annabella staring at him, her eyes wide.

"I don't know what to do," she said. "I feel so foolish, Terry. My dress, our clothes, I mean, how do they get off so that . . . oh, dear."

"Relax," he said, pulling her into his arms. "It's okay. We'll go slow and easy. Annabella, your innocence is a precious gift that I cherish. There's nothing foolish about it. If I do anything that upsets you, say so, and we'll talk about it. All right?"

She nodded. He kissed her. She melted against him, and the next thing she knew, her dress was sliding from her body and pooling at her feet. Of their own volition, it seemed, her hands slid up his chest and fumbled with the buttons on his shirt, undoing them one by one. In a mist of desire that was accompanied by murmured words and heated kisses, their clothes seemed to float away.

Annabella stood naked before him, as he stood naked before her.

"Oh, Terry," she said, her gaze moving slowly over him, "you're so beautiful, so magnificent."

"You're the beautiful one," he said, his voice husky. "You can see how much I want you, Annabella, but I won't rush you, I swear it."

He lifted her into his arms and kissed her deeply before laying her on the bed and stretching out next to her. He pulled the ribbon from her hair, then drew his fingers through the silken waves.

"Beautiful," he said again.

His mouth melted over hers.

She should be frightened, Annabella thought foggily. He was so big, so powerful, and he was going to . . . why wasn't she frightened? Because she loved him, pure and simple. Because she loved and trusted him. Because he was Terry.

Terry laid his hand on her flat stomach, then lifted his head. "Annabella, I'm going to take care of protecting you. Please don't think I was taking anything for granted because I came prepared tonight. All I knew was how much I love you and want you, and—"

"I understand, I really do."

"Lord, I love you so much."

And I love you, her heart whispered. *I love you, Terry Russell.*

As Terry took possession of her mouth once again, his hand moved upward to gently cup her breast, his thumb stroking the nipple to a hard button.

Oh, yes, Annabella thought. She'd waited for the feel of his hands on her breasts, ached for this moment. It was heavenly.

Where his hands had been, his mouth followed, and Annabella sighed in pure pleasure. He drew the soft flesh of her breast deep into his mouth, suckling in a sweet rhythm. Deep, deep within her, a matching pulse thrummed with need, and heat, and a liquid fire that seemed to be consuming her. Sensations like none she'd known or ever imagined swept through her as Terry worked his magic.

On he went, stroking, caressing, kissing, touching, until she was calling his name in a voice she didn't recognize as her own.

"Terry, please."

"Soon."

"I feel so strange. Wonderful, but strange and . . . oh, please."

His hand skimmed lower, lower, finding her, touching her. She gasped in shock, then relaxed. Trusting. Savoring. Wanting.

"Oh, Annabella, you are so ready for me," Terry said, his voice gritty with passion. "You do want me."

"Yes, yes."

"Listen to me."

"What?"

"Listen, please, Annabella. The first time isn't always terrific. I'll try not to hurt you, but . . . I promise you that later it will be wonderful. You've got to trust me about this."

"Terry, why are you talking so much?"

He smiled. "Because I'm holding onto my control by a thread, and I'm a nervous wreck because . . . any other questions?"

"No. Except—could you love me now, please?"

"Oh, Annabella," he said with a groan, then kissed her.

He lifted his head, sweat beading his brow as he slowly, oh, so slowly, entered her. He watched her face, his muscles trembling from forced restraint. Deeper he went until nature's barrier stopped him.

"I love you, Annabella. Hold onto me. Move with me, come with me to a very special place. This is the dance of lovers. Our dance."

And it began.

With instincts as old as the creation of woman

herself, Annabella followed the tempo Terry set, matched his rhythm of the dance in perfect synchronization. He went deeper within her, filling her, and she received all of him. Sensations gathered heavy within her—pulling, swirling, tightening, searching.

"Terry?"

"Yes, that's it. That's it. Move with me. Go with it, Annabella. Take it all."

She found what she was seeking as she reached the crescendo of the dance.

"Oh, Terry!"

A moment later a groan of pleasure rumbled up from his chest as he joined her in the place where she had gone. He collapsed against her, breathing heavily, burying his face in her hair.

Annabella wrapped her arms around his sweat-soaked back and held him tightly, savoring his weight, never wanting to let him go. A soft smile formed on her lips and she sighed in contentment.

Terry lifted his head. "I'm too heavy for you."

"Oh, no, please don't go."

He shifted most of his weight to his forearms. "Annabella?"

"It was so beautiful, so wonderful, and I'm not sorry, and . . . I don't know what else to say."

He smiled at her. "I'd say you covered it quite nicely. We were terrific, together. Oh, Annabella, I'm the happiest man on earth."

He lifted himself gently away, then tucked her close to his side. Annabella fiddled with the moist curls on his chest. When she discovered his nipples, he sucked in his breath.

"Careful there, ma'am, or you'll have me all over you again."

"Okay."

He chuckled. "Give your little body a break. The night is young."

"Mmm," Annabella said, then yawned. "I feel so . . . I don't know . . . sort of heavy, like I may never move again. It's a lovely feeling."

"Sleep," he said, then kissed her on the forehead.

"Just for a few minutes. If you're the happiest man on earth, then I'm the happiest woman." Her lashes drifted down.

"Good, I'm glad you're happy," he said softly. They'd work it all out. She was his now, the future was theirs. She hadn't said that she loved him, but he knew she did, or she never would have given herself to him. Yes, they'd work it all out, find all the answers they needed. They had to because he loved her, and he had no intention of letting her go. Not ever.

Nine

At midnight, to Terry's surprise and total delight, he was awakened by the tantalizing sensation of soft fingers trailing across his chest. He blinked away the fogginess of sleep and chuckled.

"Was there . . . um . . . something you wanted, Miss Annabella?" he said smiling at her.

"You," she said.

He turned over and looked at her. Her hair was a wild tumble, her cheeks were flushed with sleep. In the glow from the living room lamp that was still on, he could see her so clearly. His beautiful Annabella.

"Love me, Terry," she whispered as her hands skimmed down his sides, then over his buttocks, pressing him to her. She lifted her hips enticingly, invitingly, and Terry groaned.

"Annabella, what are you—"

"Love me."

Go slow. You mustn't hurt her, he reminded himself fiercely.

She wiggled beneath him, her busy little hands exploring, touching, moving, igniting his passion to a burning flame.

Go . . . slow, he repeated again to himself. Go . . . oh, hell, forget it.

He surged into her, his control gone, and Annabella wrapped her legs around his thighs and held him to her. The purr of pleasure that whispered from her lips was his final undoing, and he plunged deeper, filling her, then began to move. He thundered within her like a wild storm, and she met and matched his pounding rhythm. Harder. Faster. Her body tightened around him as she reached her peak, and he joined her, shuddering, trembling, calling her name.

"Annabella!"

"Yes, yes!"

He collapsed against her, gasping for breath.

"Oh, my," Annabella said dreamily, "that was lovely."

"Lovely?" he said, with a hoot of laughter. "That was wild stuff, lady."

"Didn't you like it?"

"I loved it. You're a quick study, Annabella. I didn't hurt you, did I?"

"Oh, no, not at all."

"Lord, you're fantastic, unbelievable. I love you so much."

"Oh, Terry, I"—she sighed—"I love you too."

He leveled himself up on one arm and looked at her, gently brushing her damp hair away from her face.

"Do you?" he said quietly. "Do you really love me?"

"Oh, yes, I do."

"Why do you seem so sad about it? We love each other. That's what this is all about. I hoped that you loved me, and now you've said the words. The future is ours, Annabella Abraham. Nothing can stop us now."

"But—"

"No, don't spoil this moment, okay? I realize we have things to discuss and work out. I live in New York, you're here, but we'll find all the answers, you'll see. We'll talk about everything, including why you were crying when you first came home."

"Terry, I—"

"Shh, no, not tonight. Listen to me. There's nothing I want more than to wake up next to you at dawn and make love to you again. But this isn't the time. If one of your neighbors sees me leaving here early, it will be all over town that I spent the night with you. I don't want you to be the center of any more gossip. They're already buzzing about us. Will you be okay if I go?"

"Yes, I'm sleepy."

He kissed her deeply, then slid off the bed and dressed. He leaned over her again for another searing kiss.

"I love you," he said, close to her lips. "I'll see you soon."

"I love you too. I just couldn't go another minute without telling you."

"I'm glad you did. Annabella, take this thought into your dreams. I want you to marry me. I want you to be my wife, my partner, my other half, the mother of my child."

Annabella opened her mouth, her eyes wide, but

before she could gather enough air into her lungs to speak, Terry was gone. He turned off the light in the living room, and the next sound she heard was the quiet shutting of the front door.

"Oh, Annabella," she whispered to the darkness, "he just asked you to marry him." Marry him. Marry him? Be his wife and the mother of his baby? How glorious, how wonderful, how fantastic, how . . .

Awful.

"Oh, dear. Oh, dear. Oh, dear," she said, feeling tears threatening. How could she marry Terry Russell when she didn't even know who she really was? *She* didn't know, so she also didn't know which Annabella he'd asked to marry him! All the changes, which now included having made love for the first time, were intertwined with Terry. She, herself, the person, the woman, was in there somewhere, but where? And if she found her, whom would she find? If left on her own, if there were no Terry in her life, who would she be? The old Annabella or the new?

"Dammit!" she said, punching her pillow. "Annabella Abraham, watch your mouth." Maybe, she thought frantically, it didn't matter who she really was. Terry wanted to marry her, so she'd just be the person she became when she was with him, and that would be that.

No, she thought an instant later, that wasn't honest, it wasn't real. It wouldn't be fair to Terry for her to find her real self after they were married. Somehow she had to unravel the jumble of confusion within her and find out once and for all who she was. Somehow.

With a wobbly sigh Annabella rolled onto her stomach, closed her eyes, and slept.

* * *

Terry walked slowly along the sidewalk, his hands shoved into the back pockets of his jeans, a deep frown on his face. The sounds of the summer night were drowned out by the multitude of voices shouting in his mind.

It was almost perfect, he thought. Almost, but not quite. He loved Annabella, and she loved him. She gave herself to him in passionate abandon, just as he'd known she would. But the questioning voices inside his head wouldn't leave him alone. He wanted to pretend that Annabella hadn't cried, that Annabella hadn't said that she didn't know who she was. He wanted to pretend that he didn't know what she'd meant by that.

But he did know, he admitted, and it was all his fault. The changes. If only he'd left it alone, not pushed her. There was no doubt in his mind that he would have fallen in love with the little sparrow just as she'd been the first time he'd seen her. But now, because of him, there were two Annabellas, and it was perfectly clear to him why she was confused, why she didn't know who she really was.

But which Annabella loved him?

"Oh, God," he said, running his hand down his face. What if none of this was real? What if the pretty, free-spirited Annabella, the Annabella who made love to him, was someone he had created, molded, and transformed to his specifications? What if, left on her own, Annabella sighed with relief and returned to the world of the little sparrow, wishing only to be left alone to live her life as it had been?

Of course she was confused, dammit. He'd hardly

given her a moment's peace, a chance to think for herself, since he'd met her. Now, just to muddle her mind some more, he'd asked her to marry him! What was he going to do? What if she sorted it all out, saw exactly what he'd done, then came to the conclusion that . . . oh no, what if he lost her?

No! his mind thundered. He couldn't let that happen. He was going to grab her and run, marry her before she came out of the ether and . . . But that wasn't the answer, either, he told himself.

Terry knew he had no choice. He had to give Annabella the time and space she needed to discover her true feelings and identity. He had no choice but to step back, keep silent, and run the risk of losing the woman he loved. He had no choice, and the weight of depression settling over him was crushing.

With dragging steps and a strange aching sensation in his heart, Terry walked on through the night toward home.

Annabella opened her eyes, then lay perfectly still, taking a mental inventory of herself, starting with her naked body. She shifted slightly, and felt a soreness in places foreign and new. Visions of her exquisite lovemaking with Terry flitted into view, and a soft smile formed on her lips.

Then, slowly, tentatively, she began thinking about all that had happened. She was fearful of what cold, hard facts her inner thoughts might force her to face. The hours while she'd slept since making love with Terry, since Terry had asked her to marry him, had brought no miraculous, gift-wrapped answers. The only thing that was crystal clear was that her love for Terry encompassed both Annabellas. That was comforting, but it wasn't enough to whisk the confusion into oblivion.

Annabella sighed, decided the sad sound was becoming all too familiar, and headed for the shower. She washed her hair, then allowed the water to beat against her tender breasts, savoring the memories of the feel of Terry's hands and mouth on her soft flesh. She blow-dried her hair, pulled on her underwear, and opened her closet.

She'd wear the burnt orange dress, she decided. She'd even go so far as to leave her hair totally loose. Somewhere in her dresser there was a tube of lip gloss and a bottle of cologne she could use. She'd put on her new high heels, and she'd be stunningly sophisticated, and raise the eyebrows of the citizens of Harmony, Oklahoma, another notch.

Then she'd look in the mirror and try to keep from crying as she wondered who in heaven's name she was.

Annabella carried out her plan with a feeling of detachment, as though she were watching someone else getting all gussied up. She settled into her rocker with a cup of spiced-apple tea and sipped it as she rocked slowly back and forth.

Then, with an ache in her heart and a sadness greater than any she'd ever known, she knew what she had to do.

She sipped her tea, and rocked in her rocker, as tears streamed down her cheeks.

• • •

At ten o'clock that morning Terry received a call from Houston Tyler. The executives at St. John Enterprises were definitely interested in the Cessna, he told Terry. The plane had originally been worth around thirty thousand dollars, and if it was in as good condition as Terry claimed, they were willing to pay twenty thousand for it.

"That's fair," Terry said, nodding. "It's a honey of an aircraft, but it is several years old."

"Thing is, Terry," Houston said, "these guys are tied up in a complicated merger and can't get out there right now to test-fly it. Can you sit on this for awhile? Not offer the plane to anyone else?"

"Sure. That's no problem. I'll just . . ." Terry stopped speaking and ran his fingertips over his forehead, which was throbbing painfully. "Houston, I think I'll fly the plane to New York, and let them test it there."

"Hey, you're on vacation. You don't have to do that."

"Yes," Terry said quietly, "I do."

"This has nothing to do with the plane, does it? It's your lady, right?"

"Yeah."

"You want to leave there? Leave *her*?"

"No, but I have to. It's so damned complicated, Houston, because I've screwed this up very badly. I love her, she loves me, yet I have to get out of her way for awhile, to give her some time and space."

"Why? You just said you love each other."

"As I said, it's a complicated mess."

"Terry, would you like to talk this over with January? Women understand other women, even though there are times when men don't understand women at all. Hell, January can tell what's wrong with Julie from the way the baby cries. Me? I jump and run if that little bundle even squeaks. Women are amazing. Do you think January could help you?"

"Houston, if January knew what I've done, she'd string me up by the thumbs. I've played the role of the pushy, macho, chauvinistic hotshot to the hilt. To the point, in fact, where it could very well cause me to lose Annabella."

"That bad, huh?"

"That bad."

"I don't know what to say. You really sound awful."

"That's the truth. I'll fly the Cessna up there, Houston, and I'll call you when I get in. I have to talk to Annabella before I leave, even though I don't know what I'm going to say to her. I've pressured her enough. If I make it sound like she's on a timetable to figure herself out while I'm gone, I'll only make it worse. Maybe it would be better to keep my mouth shut for a change."

"You've lost me."

"Yeah, I know, I'm blithering. I'll call you when I get to New York."

"I'll have a bottle of expensive whiskey waiting for you."

"You do that. I'll need it."

During the drive to the library Annabella began to formulate in her mind the words she would say to Terry. As she greeted Mrs. Perdy, then began her routine work, the words buzzed and hummed, pulling her attention away from what she was doing.

She escaped to her office with the mumbled excuse that she had to place an order for new books.

Sinking into the chair at her desk, she pressed her fingertips to her temples, willing the words to stop their clamor and settle into a sensible order.

How, she wondered dismally, did she say it? How did she tell the man she loved that she desperately needed some time away from him? How did she explain, make him understand, without hurting him, without losing his love?

"Dear heaven," she whispered, "I don't know." Terry had asked her to marry him, told her to think about his proposal. He was picturing a future for the two of them, and she was about to tell him she needed, *had to have*, some space, some time, alone. She didn't want to sound like a flaky woman in the midst of an overly dramatic identity crisis. Oh, she hated this, she really did.

"Annabella."

She jumped in her chair and looked up to see Terry standing in the doorway to her office.

No, no, she thought frantically, not yet, she wasn't ready yet! The words were still flying around in her head in no order. She couldn't talk to him, couldn't tell him now. Not yet!

"Annabella, I need to speak to you," he said. He stepped inside the room and closed the door behind him. "Mrs. Perdy said she'd take care of things out front. May I sit down?"

Unable to speak, Annabella nodded and motioned to the chair next to her desk. Terry pulled it out and placed it beside her. When he sat down, she swiveled in her chair to face him.

Hello, my love, her heart whispered.

Ah, Annabella, Terry thought. He couldn't lose her. He loved her! "How are you?" he said quietly.

"Fine."

"Good," he said, nodding. She looked beautiful, but he knew he mustn't comment, mustn't place any importance on her appearance.

He'd like her hair loose the way it was, Annabella thought. He'd tell her that now and also say how pretty she was in the burnt orange dress. He was looking at her, liking what he saw, and now he'd say . . .

"Annabella, it's about the airplane."

She blinked. "Pardon me?"

"You know I have potential buyers for it in New York, a couple of executives from St. John Enterprises. They were going to come out and test-fly it, but they got tied up. So . . ." He stopped speaking. *Say it, Russell*, he told himself. *Tell her you're leaving*. Dammit, do it! "I'm flying the plane to them."

"You're leaving?" she said, hardly above a whisper.

Terry slouched back in the chair and crossed his arms in a relaxed fashion over his chest. "I don't want to lose this deal. Besides"—he forced a smile that felt as phony as a three-dollar bill—"how can I resist the chance to fly that sweet machine across the country? If things go as expected, you should make twenty thousand before taxes. Not bad, huh?"

"You're leaving?" Annabella repeated.

"I'll be back . . . whenever," he said, lifting one shoulder in a shrug. "I'll bring back the papers for your signature and, of course, the check from the sale. I'm not sure how long I'll be gone. Just don't have a clue."

"I see," she said, nodding slowly. But she didn't see, she didn't understand at all! What was he really saying, what was happening here? This was the man who'd asked her to marry him? The man who'd made exquisite love to her? He was leaving, now, because he couldn't resist the chance to fly an airplane? What about them? Had it all been an act, a vacation fling, to Terry? Was he snickering over his grand seduction of the old maid librarian and bailing out now before things got sticky?

Terry slapped his hands onto his thighs and pushed himself to his feet. "Well, I've got to go. The blue heavens are calling my name. We'll . . . um . . . talk when I get back. You know, discuss what . . . needs to be discussed. Right?"

"Right," she said, staring up at him with wide eyes.

"You can think about . . . things while I'm gone. Right?"

"Right."

"Good." He leaned over and brushed his lips across hers. "See ya." He straightened, then strode to the door. He hesitated a moment, then yanked the door open and went out, not closing it behind him.

Annabella stared at the empty doorway, her heart racing as a shiver coursed through her. She closed her eyes for a moment as a shattering pain rippled through her body.

Terry was gone.

With an attitude as casual as someone talking about the weather, he was walking—no, flying—out of her life, she realized incredulously. He was the traveling salesman, she was the stupid, naive farmer's daughter. She couldn't believe this! He'd be back, he'd said. No, he wouldn't. He'd mail the check, the papers, whatever was necessary for the sale of the plane.

Terry Russell was gone.

He'd come to Harmony, he'd seen her, he'd conquered her. And now it was over. The pain, the hurt, the sense of betrayal felt like more than she could bear. She loved him!

Annabella slammed the door on her screaming thoughts, narrowed her eyes, and got slowly to her feet.

Terry Russell was, she thought, the most despicable man she'd ever met. He was a user, a taker, a lowlife in its purest form. Not one tear—not one! —was she going to shed. No, sir. She had lived, and she had learned, and for two cents she'd strangle him with her bare hands. Yes, she loved him, but she'd get over him. She was Annabella Abraham, and a . . . a reprobate, a rogue, a playboy like Mr. Russell was not going to be her undoing. Right?

"Right!" she said, smacking the desk with her hand. Tears spilled onto her cheeks and she brushed them angrily away. She was back in control of her life, dammit. Dammit? she questioned. Yes, dammit.

With a toss of her head and her nose in the air, Annabella marched out of the office.

"Everything all right, Miss Annabella?" Mrs. Perdy said.

"Call me Annabella," she said firmly. "From now on, everyone will call me Annabella."

"Oh, well, that's mighty friendly of you," Mrs. Perdy said. "That is such a pretty dress you're wearing."

Annabella looked down at the soft burnt orange material. "This dress? Well, I haven't decided if I like it. I didn't have a chance, you see, to really think about it before I bought it. There are, in fact, a great many things I intend to make decisions on."

"Is that a fact?" Mrs. Perdy said. "Like what?"

"My life, Mrs. Perdy. My life, and the choices available to me. I plan to discover just who I am." She pointed a finger in the air. "Annabella Abraham has spoken!"

Annabella decided that she had made it through the day like a champ. She had apologized to Ralph Newberry for hollering at him to blow his nose, told him to call her Annabella from that day forward, then had watched in dismay as he dissolved in a coughing, sneezing, runny-nose fit. She had handed him a box of tissues, patted him on the arm, and left him and his nose at a far corner table in the library.

She then called Esther Sue to tell her that she would not be providing homemade bread and sugar tea-cookies for the bake sale at the church on Sunday. She would, Annabella stated, bring a triple batch of fudge brownies. Why? Because, she informed Esther Sue, it was time for a change.

"Well, that's fine . . . I guess, Miss Annabella," Esther Sue said. "Yes, of course, it is."

"Call me Annabella."

"Indeed I will. Thank you . . . Annabella."

After work Annabella went to the beauty shop. Her instructions were clear. She wanted to wear her hair loose and free, but it needed trimming and shaping.

The young girl snipped away without losing any of the length of Annabella's hair, and the result was a shiny, wavy, nicely styled hairdo.

"There you go, Miss Annabella," the girl said.

"Call me Annabella," she said, and gave her a generous tip.

As Annabella drove home she had a sneaking suspicion that she was due for a long, loud cry. While her resolve to forget Terry Russell was firm, her anger perking right along, she was also very aware of the heavy ache in her heart. She had loved, and she had lost and, oh, it did hurt so very, very much.

Well, she thought ruefully, she certainly had all the time and space she needed to find out who she really was, and she hadn't said one word to Terry to get it. He had dumped her flat, leaving her with only memories. Memories, she had a feeling, she would never have the fortitude to draw from her heart, mind, and soul to relive and cherish. Memories that would best be forgotten.

And the tears did come.

At the sight of the bouquet of violets sitting in the little vase on the end table, Annabella wept. As she'd anticipated, she cried very loudly and for a very long time. And then she stopped. For the remainder of the evening, she rearranged the furniture, did not have one cup of spiced-apple tea, and purposely waited until eleven o'clock before going to bed.

Changes, she thought, staring up into the darkness. Oh, yes, she was making them. But they were hers and hers alone, things *she* wanted to do because they felt right. *Because it was who she was!*

•   •   •

The moment of truth came at dawn the next morning.

It came as Annabella stood in front of her open closet door.

She stood there wrapped in a towel, her gaze sweeping back and forth between the pretty new clothes hanging on the left and her old wardrobe on the right. She looked at the clothes at the same time she was looking deep within herself for the answers she sought.

And then, with a sudden sense of peace, of calmness, with a feeling she could only describe as coming home—coming home to herself, to who she was, the woman she was meant to be—Annabella Abraham reached in the closet and took from a hanger the black-and-white-striped dress that should have made her look like a zebra but didn't.

Before leaving for work, she stood in front of the full-length mirror. "Hello, Annabella Abraham," she said softly. "You're a bit late getting here, but you finally arrived." She paused and swallowed a tiny sob that caught in her throat. "And thank you, Terry Russell, you rat. I'll figure out how to stop loving you, somehow. But I do thank you for giving me . . . me."

A week passed.

Then two.

Annabella donated her old wardrobe to the church for their annual rummage sale, then drove to Tulsa for another shopping spree. Her closet overflowed with lovely clothes in bright, happy colors. Slowly but surely people became comfortable calling her Annabella. She had lunch with Clara and Susie, quit the Quilting Club, and became a member of the Square Dance Swingers.

And every night she dreamed of Terry.

No amount of firm lectures to herself before going to bed at eleven or twelve, or whenever the mood struck, stopped the image of Terry from floating through her nights. She resigned herself to his nocturnal visits and to the tearstained pillow she often found upon awakening. She still loved him, she knew, and maybe she always would. It was, perhaps, the price she would pay for having at last become the woman she was meant to be.

When Terry had been gone for three weeks, it suddenly occurred to Annabella that he had spoken of her receiving twenty thousand dollars for the airplane. Surely, she told herself, he hadn't absconded with her funds. Not Terry, not the son of dear Mary and Mike Russell. Whatever else Terry might be, he couldn't be a thief as well.

But, she wondered, why hadn't he sent the check and the papers for her to sign? She didn't expect him to show his face in Harmony, but where was her money?

At the end of the fourth week Annabella had had enough. She picked up the telephone, dialed information, and asked for the number of St. John Enterprises in New York. With a trembling hand she dialed the number she was given.

"St. John Enterprises."

"May I speak to Terry Russell, please?"

"Terry . . . may I ask who's calling?"

"Miss Annabella Abraham," she said, lifting her chin.

"Well, Mr. Russell can be reached at another number. Do you have a pencil?"

"Yes, go ahead."

A few minutes later Annabella dialed again.

"Hello?" a woman said.

A woman? Annabella thought miserably. He already had another woman. "Terry Russell, please."

"May I ask—"

"Miss Annabella Abraham," she interrupted.

"At last," the woman mumbled.

"Pardon me?"

"Nothing. Annabella . . . may I call you Annabella? I feel as though I know you. This is January St. John Tyler. Terry is a close friend of mine and of my husband's, Houston."

"Oh," Annabella said, not knowing what else to say.

"It is such a pleasure to get to say hello to you."

It was? Annabella thought. This conversation wasn't making any sense. "Is Terry there, please?" She had to get this over with.

"No," January said, "he's out fishing. You're calling January Hall, Houston's and my home off the coast of Maine. Terry just loves to fish here. May I give him a message?"

"Yes, if you will. Would you please tell Mr. Russell that Miss Annabella Abraham called regarding the status of my funds from the sale of the airplane? Or the status of the plane itself? If he has time to fish, he most certainly has time to tend to business."

"I thoroughly agree with you, Annabella," January

said decisively. "I'll give Terry your message the minute I see him."

"Thank you, Mrs. Tyler."

"January. Please do call me January."

"Well, thank you for your help . . . January. Goodbye."

"Ta-ta," January said cheerfully. She hung up the receiver and spun around to smile at Houston and Terry. "Jackpot."

"Oh, Lord," Terry said, running his hand over the back of his neck, "this is it. I sure hope you know what we're doing, January."

"Sweetheart, trust me," she said. "I understand women."

"She does, she does," Houston said. "She even understands herself, which really takes some doing."

January laughed. "Houston, hush. Terry, from everything you told me, Annabella *had* to have this time you gave her. The tricky part was to know when to go back to Harmony. Women, geniuses that we are, can sniff out a bargain a mile away. Getting the most for our money is a matter of pride. You have disappeared with what is potentially twenty thousand female dollars. The fact that all these weeks have passed, and Annabella is only now doing something about the money, says she's used her time the way you've hoped."

"She's found out who she really is," Terry said quietly.

"I'd bet on it and win," January said. "When you go back to Harmony, Terry, you'll find the real Annabella Abraham. She'll be either a fashion plate or your little sparrow."

"It doesn't matter which one she is," Terry said. "I love her. Question is, does she love *me*? Does the real Annabella love me?"

January reached up and kissed him on the cheek. "Go home to Annabella," she said softly, "and find out. Good luck, Terry."

"He's going to need all he can get," Houston said. "He's dealing with a woman."

January laughed again. "Houston, would you just hush? Terry, go pack."

"Thanks, both of you," Terry said. "You're great friends."

"Go to your lady, Terry," Houston said, "and fight like hell for her. Believe me, chum, it's worth it."

"My love," January said, throwing her arms around Houston's neck. "What a wonderful thing to say."

Terry looked at January and Houston as the couple smiled warmly, lovingly, at each other. Then he turned and walked from the room.

Ten

The night after she had spoken with January St. John Tyler on the telephone, Annabella had dreams of Terry that were even more vivid than usual. She woke often, reaching for him, then knew a tremendous sense of loss and loneliness when she found only emptiness next to her in bed.

Fortunately, the next day was Saturday, and Annabella, much to her own amazement, slept until nine o'clock instead of waking at her usual time. She'd had at least a few hours of restful sleep and decided to weed the geraniums by the front porch.

She dressed in her new, snug-fitting jeans, tennis shoes, and a bright red T-shirt with white letters across the front that said CHECK OUT A LIBRARIAN. To keep her hair out of the way while she worked, she plaited the silky tresses into two thick braids, secured at the ends with red rubber bands. Her new gardening gloves were white with bright violets. With the rather oversized gloves in place she went out the front door, filled her lungs with fresh morning air, then dropped to her knees in front of the flower beds and began to pull the weeds.

Within ten minutes Annabella knew that her mind was not going to be her best friend that morning. The red geraniums brought back memories of the Sunday she'd worn one of the pretty flowers on her dress to church. She remembered every moment, every sensation of sitting so close to Terry in that pew. She relived the kiss in broad daylight under the big tree and all that had transpired later at the man-made lake.

Annabella yanked on some weeds. It wasn't fair, she decided, that simple red flowers could trigger so many memories. Maybe she should dig up the geraniums and plant violets instead. No, violets evoked memories of Terry too. Darn it, was nothing sacred, nothing safe? Images of Terry were everywhere.

She pulled out another handful of weeds with more force than was necessary. What had been Terry's reaction, she wondered, when January had given him the message that Annabella Abraham had telephoned regarding the money from the sale of her airplane? Had he rolled his eyes in annoyance that he'd have to tend to business rather than go fishing, as he preferred to do? Well, too bad. That plane or the money was hers, and he'd fiddled around with it long enough.

So, she thought sadly, he'd stick some papers in an envelope and mail them off to her. That would be that. Final chapter, end of story.

Annabella stared at a red geranium, seeing Terry's face so clearly in the flower. "Stop that," she said, to the bright blossom. "Oh, great, now I'm talking to geraniums. Hello, weeds," she said, to the clump in her hand. "How's life?"

With a shake of her head Annabella dropped the weeds and grabbed another handful. She heard the sound of a car coming down the street, but didn't turn to look at it.

Nope, she thought. Her imagination was working overtime this morning, and no matter who was in that car, her tricky little mind would see Terry Russell for sure. She'd had enough memories since coming outside to last her a week.

Still not looking up, she realized that the car had pulled into her driveway. The car was stopping, the ignition was turned off. Door opening, shutting. She was going to peek now, see who it was. And, by golly, if she saw a vision of Terry, she was going to have herself committed.

She turned her head, let out a shriek, and spun around so fast she landed with a thud on her bottom. There she sat, legs stiff on the ground in front of her, her eyes wide, her mouth forming an astonished O. She couldn't move, could hardly breathe because . . .

Terry Russell was standing in the middle of her lawn!

Terry's heart raced, the wild pounding echoing in his ears. There she was—his love, his life, his beautiful Annabella.

And she wasn't the little sparrow.

She'd done it, he thought. She'd discovered who she was, knew her own identity, who the woman within her wanted to be. The little brown sparrow didn't wear tight jeans and a T-shirt with a double-meaning slogan. The little brown sparrow didn't fix her hair in braids and put big violet-covered gloves on her hands. This was the real Annabella. She'd found her answers. And now he had to find his.

Did the real Annabella love him?

"Hello, Annabella," he murmured.

Annabella attempted to speak, knew it was a hopeless effort, and simply nodded slightly. He was really there, she thought, her mind racing. This was true. Dressed in faded jeans and a blue shirt, he was standing in her front yard with three boxes in his arms. His tanned arms, his muscled arms. Arms that were strong, yet gentle, when he—Annabella, stop it, she ordered herself. She had to pull this off with a little dignity.

"I'd like to talk to you, Annabella," Terry said.

Annabella waved a violet-covered glove breezily in the air. "Go right ahead. Talk."

He glanced at the neighboring houses. "Could we go inside?"

"Why?"

"Because what I have to say to you is personal."

"Well, I'm terribly busy, as you can see. Weeds wait for no one, you know. They'll gobble my geraniums right up if I don't tend to them."

"Please? I won't keep you long," he said. Only for a lifetime, only for forever, he hoped.

Annabella sighed a rather bored, put-upon sigh.

She got to her feet and nearly cheered aloud when her trembling legs supported her.

"Yes, all right," she said. "Come into the living room." She marched ahead of him, braids bouncing against her breasts, her gloves still firmly in place.

Inside, Terry set the three boxes on a chair, instantly registered the fact that the furniture was rearranged, and looked intently at Annabella.

"I presume," she said, from across the room, "that you received my message and have come about my money for the plane."

"No. Yes. I mean, yes, I have a check for you for twenty thousand dollars. But, no, that's not the only reason I came. Could we sit down?"

"No."

"Wonderful," he muttered.

"Please get on with it, Mr. Russell. I'm really very busy," she said. And she was very close to tears, and he had to go. Now! She couldn't bear this. Her heart hurt, everything hurt. She wanted him to go and leave her alone once and for all. She wanted him to stay forever, never leave her again, make love to her right that minute and . . .

"Annabella."

"What!" she yelled.

"Please, could we sit down?"

Good idea, she thought rather hysterically. Her trembling legs were definitely giving up the ghost. "Well, yes, I suppose," she said, then sank gratefully into her rocker.

Terry crossed the room and sat on the sofa, which was now at a different angle than it had been before.

He leaned forward, rested his elbows on his knees, and clasped his hands loosely together as he looked directly at Annabella.

This was it, he thought. The remainder of his life was going to be determined in the next few minutes. *Oh, Lord, Annabella, please!*

"Annabella," he said, his voice slightly raspy, "I owe you an apology."

"Not necessary," she said, examining the violets on the back of one glove. "I'm a mature woman. I understand how these vacation flings work. You had one, you left." She shrugged. "People do it all the time."

"I did not," he said, straightening up on the sofa, "have a vacation fling. I'm not apologizing for having a vacation fling, because I didn't have one. Got that? And quit staring at that glove like you've never seen it before in your life. I've got something important to say here."

Annabella looked up at him. "Well! Really! You're becoming rather rude. There's no reason to raise your voice."

"Damned right, there's a reason, lady. I've gone through hell this past month, missing you, aching for you, dreaming about you. I'll yell all I want to because you've driven me right out of my mind!"

Annabella blinked. "Pardon me?"

"Oh, no," he said, dragging his hand through his hair, "I'm blowing this." He took a deep breath, then let it out slowly. "Annabella, just listen, okay?" he said softly. "I had to go. I had to give you a chance to discover who you really were. I heard you when you spoke, Annabella. I knew what I'd done. I'm apologizing for steamrolling you, for taking over your life, your choices, without giving you a chance to even think about what *you* wanted. I handled it all wrong, and I'm sorry."

"I—"

"Wait," he said, raising a hand. "Let me finish. I was convinced that you'd be happier if you made the changes I was forcing on you. Your clothes, your hair, your . . . responses to my kisses, were all new, and I'd made up my mind it was perfect for you. But I heard you, Annabella. I heard you say you didn't know who you were anymore, and I had to face what I'd done to you."

He ran his hand down his face as Annabella stared at him with wide eyes.

He continued. "I realized there were two Annabellas because of me, and you weren't sure which one you really wanted to be. And so I left you. It was the toughest thing I've ever done. I can tell that you've figured out who you are. The old Annabella wouldn't dress like you are right now. I'd bet that your closet if full of pretty clothes. Right?"

"Yes," she whispered.

"Than my leaving served its purpose. You had the time and space you needed to discover who you really are. Right?"

"Yes."

"That's good, great, but—ah, hell, Annabella, I want you to know, to believe me, trust me, when I say that I love you more than life itself. All these weeks I've hoped, prayed, that when you discovered the real you, you'd also find that that Annabella loved me. It didn't matter, don't you see? It didn't matter which one you were, as long as you loved me. Old clothes or new, hair in a bun or loose . . . ah, damn, I don't care. Nothing is important except whether or not you love me and if you'll say you'll marry me. Please, Annabella, don't make me spend the rest of my life without you. Alone. Lonely. Please?"

She was a blur of motion. She was braids flying, and tears streaming, as she ran across the room and flung herself into Terry's arms. She wrapped her great big gloves around his neck, wiggled onto his lap, and looked into his startled blue eyes.

"I thought you'd left me forever," she said, unable to control her tears. "Oh, Terry, you were right. I was so confused. But, Terry, one thing was always clear, always. Both Annabellas loved you. I was so afraid that if I found I was the old Annabella, that you wouldn't love me anymore. But then, it seemed, you didn't want either one, because you left and . . . oh, thank you. Thank you for giving me the time I needed. It was so painful, but so necessary, and I love you so very, very much."

Terry closed his eyes for a moment. "Thank God," he whispered. He opened his eyes again, giving up his battle to hide the tears shimmering in his eyes. "I love you, Annabella. Marry me. Please say you'll marry me."

"Yes, yes, yes," she said, smiling through her tears.

"Will you move to New York? We'll get a house out of the city, a place with a yard for our baby to play in. I talked to January and Houston, and I won't do the overseas flights anymore, so I won't be gone for long stretches of time. We'll find a library for you to work in, if you want to, and . . . okay?"

"Yes, yes, yes."

"Darling Annabella," he said, then brought his mouth down hard onto hers.

The kiss was long and powerful, and passions soared. The flames of desire burned into forgotten cinders the hurt and loneliness of the past weeks. There was only now, and the promise of endless tomorrows.

"I want you," Terry said, close to her lips.

"Yes, yes, yes,"

He chuckled. "Your record is stuck."

"Terry, I'm so happy. I've missed you so much. I want you too."

"Than let's go into the bedroom and . . . wait. I forgot. I brought you some presents."

Annabella slid off his lap, and watched as he retrieved the three boxes from the chair and put them on the sofa. The top one was square and he set it to one side. He took the tops off the two flat ones to reveal white tissue paper.

"I didn't know who I'd find here, Annabella," he said softly, "but I knew I loved you no matter which Annabella you were." He motioned toward the boxes.

Annabella looked at him questioningly, then brushed back the tissue in one of the boxes. It contained a chiffon dress in varying shades of purple, pink, and rose, like a gorgeous rainbow.

"It's beautiful!"

"Look in the other box," he said.

Beneath the tissue was a plain brown dress, made of expensive, heavy material. It had a Peter Pan collar, a narrow brown belt, and dark brown buttons.

"You see, Annabella? I brought gifts to my lady, whoever she was, whoever she needed, wanted, to be."

"Oh, Terry," she said, fresh tears misting her eyes again, "thank you."

"And this," he said, taking the top off the square box, "is also for you." He lifted out the treasure and held it with both hands.

It was a birthday cake.

It was covered in candy violets, had a purple candle in the middle, and said Happy Birthday, Annabella around the top edge.

Annabella gasped.

"You told me once that you'd never had a birthday cake, and had never learned how to make wishes before you blew out the candles. Now, Annabella, we'll have a lifetime of birthdays together, and you can practice making a wish on this cake."

"I think," she murmured, "that all my wishes have already come true."

"They've just begun. *We've* just begun. Let me love you now, Annabella. I need you, and want you, so much."

"Yes. Oh, yes."

He placed the cake on the end table, then circled her shoulders with his arm, and they started toward the bedroom. But then he stopped.

"Annabella, I realize that you have the right to make whatever changes you want to. That's fine, great, super. It's just that . . . well, do you think you could . . . that is . . ."

"What are you trying to say, Terry?"

"Do you think that before we make love, you could take off those nutsy gloves?"

Annabella laughed, and the gloves were dropped onto the floor. They were followed by the red T-shirt, a lacy bra, a pair of new, snug-fitting jeans, and . . .

And the world beyond the little house on Peach Street was forgotten.

THE EDITOR'S CORNER

What a wonderful summer of romance reading we have in store for you. Truly, you're going to be LOVESWEPT with some happy surprises through the long, hot, lazy days ahead.

First, you're going to get **POCKETS FULL OF JOY,** LOVESWEPT #270, by our new Canadian author, Judy Gill. Elaina McIvor wondered helplessly what she was going to do with an eleven-month-old baby to care for. Dr. "Brad" Bradshaw had been the stork and deposited the infant on her doorstep and raced away. But he was back soon enough to "play doctor" and "play house" in one of the most delightful and sensuous romances of the season.

Joan Elliott Pickart has created two of her most intriguing characters ever in **TATTERED WINGS,** LOVESWEPT #271. Devastatingly handsome Mark Hampton—an Air Force Colonel whose once exciting life now seems terribly lonely—and beautiful, enigmatic Eden Landry—a top fashion model who left her glamorous life for a secluded ranch—meet one snowy night. Desire flares immediately. But so do problems. Mark soon discovers that Eden is like a perfect butterfly encased in a cube of glass. You'll revel in the ways he finds to break down the walls without hurting the woman!

For all of you who've written to ask for Tara's and Jed's love story, here your fervent requests

(continued)

are answered with Barbara Boswell's terrific **AND TARA, TOO,** LOVESWEPT #272. As we know, Jed Ramsey is as darkly sleek and as seductive and as winning with women as a man can be. And Tara Brady wants no part of him. It would be just too convenient, she thinks, if all the Brady sisters married Ramsey men. But that's exactly what Jed's tyrannical father has in mind. You'll chuckle and gasp as Tara and Jed rattle the chains of fate in a breathlessly sensual and touching love story.

Margie McDonnell is an author who can transport you to another world. This time she takes you to **THE LAND OF ENCHANTMENT,** via LOVESWEPT #273, to meet a modern-day, ever so gallant knight, dashing Patrick Knight, and the sensitive and lovely Karen Harris. Karen is the single parent of an exceptional son and a quite sensible lady . . . until she falls for the handsome hunk who is as merry as he is creative. We think you'll delight in this very special, very thrilling love story.

It gives us enormous pleasure next month to celebrate the fifth anniversary of Iris Johansen's writing career. Her first ever published book was LOVESWEPT's **STORMY VOWS** in August 1983. With that and its companion romance **TEMPEST AT SEA,** published in September 1983, Iris launched the romance featuring spin-off and/or continuing characters. Now everyone's doing it! But, still,

(continued)

nobody does it quite like the woman who began it all, Iris Johansen. Here, next month, you'll meet old friends and new lovers in **BLUE SKIES AND SHINING PROMISES,** LOVESWEPT #274. (The following month she'll also have a LOVESWEPT, of course, and we wonder if you can guess who the featured characters will be.) Don't miss the thrilling love story of Cameron Bandor (yes, you know him) and Damita Shaughnessy, whose background will shock, surprise and move you, taking you right back to five years ago!

Welcome, back, Peggy Webb! In the utterly bewitching LOVESWEPT #275, **SLEEPLESS NIGHTS,** Peggy tells the story of Tanner Donovan of the quicksilver eyes and Amanda Lassiter of the tart tongue and tender heart. In this thrilling and sensuous story, you have a marvelous battle of wits between lovers parted in the past and determined to best each other in the present. A real delight!

As always, we hope that not one of our LOVE-SWEPTs will ever disappoint you. Enjoy!

Carolyn Nichols

Carolyn Nichols
  Editor
LOVESWEPT
Bantam Books
666 Fifth Avenue
New York, NY 10103

THE HOMETOWN HUNK CONTEST

**FOR EVERY WOMAN WHO HAS EVER SAID—
"I know a man who looks
just like the hero of this book"
—HAVE WE GOT A CONTEST FOR YOU!**

To help celebrate our fifth year of publishing LOVESWEPT we are having a fabulous, fun-filled event called THE HOMETOWN HUNK contest. We are going to reissue six classic early titles by six of your favorite authors.

DARLING OBSTACLES by Barbara Boswell
IN A CLASS BY ITSELF by Sandra Brown
C.J.'S FATE by Kay Hooper
THE LADY AND THE UNICORN by Iris Johansen
CHARADE by Joan Elliott Pickart
FOR THE LOVE OF SAMI by Fayrene Preston

Here, as in the backs of all July, August, and September 1988 LOVESWEPTS you will find "cover notes" just like the ones we prepare at Bantam as the background for our art director to create our covers. These notes will describe the hero and heroine, give a teaser on the plot, and suggest a scene for the cover. Your part in the contest will be to see if a great looking local man—or men, if your hometown is so blessed—fits our description of one of the heroes of the six books we will reissue.

THE HOMETOWN HUNK who is selected (one for each of the six titles) will be flown to New York via United Airlines and will stay at the Loews Summit Hotel—the ideal hotel for business or pleasure in midtown Manhattan—for two nights. All travel arrangements made by Reliable Travel International, Incorporated. He will be the model for the new cover of the book which will be released in mid-1989. The six people who send in the winning photos of their HOMETOWN HUNK will receive a pre-selected assortment of LOVESWEPT books free for one year. Please see the Official Rules above the Official Entry Form for full details and restrictions.

We can't wait to start judging those pictures! Oh, and you must let the man you've chosen know that you're entering him in the contest. After all, if he wins he'll have to come to New York.

Have fun. Here's your chance to get the cover-lover of your dreams!

Carolyn Nichols

Carolyn Nichols
Editor
LOVESWEPT
Bantam Books
666 Fifth Avenue
New York, NY 10102–0023

THE HOMETOWN HUNK CONTEST

DARLING OBSTACLES
(Originally Published as LOVESWEPT #95)
By Barbara Boswell

COVER NOTES

The Characters:

Hero:
GREG WILDER's gorgeous body and "to-die-for" good looks
haven't hurt him in the dating department, but when
most women discover he's a widower with four kids, they
head for the hills! Greg has the hard, muscular build of an
athlete, and his light brown hair, which he wears neatly
parted on the side, is streaked blond by the sun. Add to
that his aquamarine blue eyes that sparkle when he laughs,
and his sensual mouth and generous lower lip, and you're
probably wondering what woman in her right mind
wouldn't want Greg's strong, capable surgeon's hands working their magic on her—kids or no kids!

Personality Traits:
An acclaimed neurosurgeon, Greg Wilder is a celebrity of
sorts in the planned community of Woodland, Maryland.
Authoritative, debonair, self-confident, his reputation for
engaging in one casual relationship after another almost
overshadows his prowess as a doctor. In reality, Greg
dates more out of necessity than anything else, since he
has to attend one social function after another. He con-
siders most of the events boring and wishes he could
spend more time with his children. But his profession is a
difficult and demanding one—and being both father and
mother to four kids isn't any less so. A thoughtful, generous, sometimes befuddled father, Greg tries to do it all.
Cerebral, he uses his intellect and skill rather than physical
strength to win his victories. However, he never expected
to come up against one Mary Magdalene May!

Heroine:
MARY MAGDALENE MAY, called Maggie by her friends, is the thirty-two-year-old mother of three children. She has shoulder-length auburn hair, and green eyes that shout her Irish heritage. With high cheekbones and an upturned nose covered with a smattering of freckles, Maggie thinks of herself more as the girl-next-door type. Certainly, she believes, she could never be one of Greg Wilder's beautiful escorts.

Setting: The small town of Woodland, Maryland

The Story:
Surgeon Greg Wilder wanted to court the feisty and beautiful widow who'd been caring for his four kids, but she just wouldn't let him past her doorstep! Sure that his interest was only casual, and that he preferred more sophisticated women, Maggie May vowed to keep Greg at arm's length. But he wouldn't take no for an answer. And once he'd crashed through her defenses and pulled her into his arms, he was tireless—and reckless—in his campaign to win her over. Maggie had found it tough enough to resist one determined doctor; now he threatened to call in his kids and hers as reinforcements—seven rowdy snags to romance!

Cover scene:
As if romancing Maggie weren't hard enough, Greg can't seem to find time to spend with her without their children around. Stealing a private moment on the stairs in Maggie's house, Greg and Maggie embrace. She is standing one step above him, but she still has to look up at him to see into his eyes. Greg's hands are on her hips, and her hands are resting on his shoulders. Maggie is wearing a very sheer, short pink nightgown, and Greg has on wheat-colored jeans and a navy and yellow striped rugby shirt. Do they have time to kiss?

THE HOMETOWN HUNK CONTEST

IN A CLASS BY ITSELF
(Originally Published as LOVESWEPT #66)
By Sandra Brown

COVER NOTES

The Characters:

Hero:
LOGAN WEBSTER would have no trouble posing for a Scandinavian travel poster. His wheat-colored hair always seems to be tousled, defying attempts to control it, and falls across his wide forehead. Thick eyebrows one shade darker than his hair accentuate his crystal blue eyes. He has a slender nose that flairs slightly over a mouth that testifies to both sensitivity and strength. The faint lines around his eyes and alongside his mouth give the impression that reaching the ripe age of 30 wasn't all fun and games for him. Logan's square, determined jaw is punctuated by a vertical cleft. His broad shoulders and narrow waist add to his tall, lean appearance.

Personality traits:
Logan Webster has had to scrape and save and fight for everything he's gotten. Born into a poor farm family, he was driven to succeed and overcome his "wrong side of the tracks" image. His businesses include cattle, real estate, and natural gas. Now a pillar of the community, Logan's life has been a true rags-to-riches story. Only Sandra Brown's own words can describe why he is masculinity epitomized: "Logan had 'the walk,' that saddle-tramp saunter that was inherent to native Texan men, passed down through generations of cowboys. It was, without even trying to be, sexy. The unconscious roll of the hips, the slow strut, the flexed knees, the slouching stance, the deceptive laziness that hid a latent aggressiveness." Wow! And not only does he have "the walk," but he's fun

and generous and kind. Even with his wealth, he feels at home living in his small hometown with simple, hard-working, middle-class, backbone-of-America folks. A born leader, people automatically gravitate toward him.

Heroine:
DANI QUINN is a sophisticated twenty-eight-year-old woman. Dainty, her body compact, she is utterly feminine. Dani's pale, lustrous hair is moonlight and honey spun together, and because it is very straight, she usually wears it in a chignon. With golden eyes to match her golden hair, Dani is the one woman Logan hasn't been able to get off his mind for the ten years they've been apart.

Setting: Primarily on Logan's ranch in East Texas.

The Story:
Ten years had passed since Dani Quinn had graduated from high school in the small Texas town, ten years since the night her elopement with Logan Webster had ended in disaster. Now Dani approached her tenth reunion with uncertainty. Logan would be there . . . Logan, the only man who'd ever made her shiver with desire and need, but would she have the courage to face the fury in his eyes? She couldn't defend herself against his anger and hurt—to do so would demand she reveal the secret sorrow she shared with no one. Logan's touch had made her his so long ago. Could he reach past the pain to make her his for all time?

Cover Scene:
It's sunset, and Logan and Dani are standing beside the swimming pool on his ranch, embracing. The pool is surrounded by semitropical plants and lush flower beds. In the distance, acres of rolling pasture land resembling a green lake undulate into dense, piney woods. Dani is wearing a strapless, peacock blue bikini and sandals with leather ties that wrap around her ankles. Her hair is straight and loose, falling to the middle of her back. Logan has on a light-colored pair of corduroy shorts and a short-sleeved designer knit shirt in a pale shade of yellow.

THE HOMETOWN HUNK CONTEST

C.J.'S FATE
(Originally Published as LOVESWEPT #32)
By Kay Hooper

COVER NOTES

The Characters:

Hero:
FATE WESTON easily could have walked straight off an Indian reservation. His raven black hair and strong, well-molded features testify to his heritage. But somewhere along the line genetics threw Fate a curve—his eyes are the deepest, darkest blue imaginable! Above those blue eyes are dark slanted eyebrows, and fanning out from those eyes are faint laugh lines—the only sign of the fact that he's thirty-four years old. Tall, Fate moves with easy, loose-limbed grace. Although he isn't an athlete, Fate takes very good care of himself, and it shows in his strong physique. Striking at first glance and fascinating with each succeeding glance, the serious expressions on his face make him look older than his years, but with one smile he looks boyish again.

Personality traits:
Fate possesses a keen sense of humor. His heavy-lidded, intelligent eyes are capable of concealment, but there is a shrewdness in them that reveals the man hadn't needed college or a law degree to be considered intelligent. The set of his head tells you that he is proud—perhaps even a bit arrogant. He is attractive and perfectly well aware of that fact. Unconventional, paradoxical, tender, silly, lusty, gentle, comical, serious, absurd, and endearing are all words that come to mind when you think of Fate. He is not ashamed to be everything a man can be. A defense attorney by profession, one can detect a bit of frustrated actor in his character. More than anything else, though, it's the

impression of humor about him—reinforced by the elusive dimple in his cheek—that makes Fate Weston a scrumptious hero!

Heroine:
C.J. ADAMS is a twenty-six-year-old research librarian. Unaware of her own attractiveness, C.J. tends to play down her pixylike figure and tawny gold eyes. But once she meets Fate, she no longer feels that her short, burnished copper curls and the sprinkling of freckles on her nose make her unappealing. He brings out the vixen in her, and changes the smart, bookish woman who professed to have no interest in men into the beautiful, sexy woman she really was all along. Now, if only he could get her to tell him what C.J. stands for!

Setting: Ski lodge in Aspen, Colorado

The Story:
C.J. Adams had been teased enough about her seeming lack of interest in the opposite sex. On a ski trip with her five best friends, she impulsively embraced a handsome stranger, pretending they were secret lovers—and the delighted lawyer who joined in her impetuous charade seized the moment to deepen the kiss. Astonished at his reaction, C.J. tried to nip their romance in the bud—but found herself nipping at his neck instead! She had met her match in a man who could answer her witty remarks with clever ripostes of his own, and a lover whose caresses aroused in her a passionate need she'd never suspected that she could feel. Had destiny somehow tossed them together?

Cover Scene:
C.J. and Fate virtually have the ski slopes to themselves early one morning, and they take advantage of it! Frolicking in a snow drift, Fate is covering C.J. with snow—and kisses! They are flushed from the cold weather and from the excitement of being in love. C.J. is wearing a sky-blue, one-piece, tight-fitting ski outfit that zips down the front. Fate is wearing a navy blue parka and matching ski pants.

THE HOMETOWN HUNK CONTEST

THE LADY AND THE UNICORN
(Originally Published as LOVESWEPT #29)
By Iris Johansen

COVER NOTES

The Characters:

Hero:
Not classically handsome, RAFE SANTINE's blunt, craggy features reinforce the quality of overpowering virility about him. He has wide, Slavic cheekbones and a bold, thrusting chin, which give the impression of strength and authority. Thick black eyebrows are set over piercing dark eyes. He wears his heavy, dark hair long. His large frame measures in at almost six feet four inches, and it's hard to believe that a man with such brawny shoulders and strong thighs could exhibit the pantherlike grace which characterizes Rafe's movements. Rafe Santine is definitely a man to be reckoned with, and heroine Janna Cannon does just that!

Personality traits:
Our hero is a man who radiates an aura of power and danger, and women find him intriguing and irresistible. Rafe Santine is a self-made billionaire at the age of thirty-eight. Almost entirely self-educated, he left school at sixteen to work on his first construction job, and by the time he was twenty-three, he owned the company. From there he branched out into real estate, computers, and oil. Rafe reportedly changes mistresses as often as he changes shirts. His reputation for ruthless brilliance has been earned over years of fighting to the top of the economic ladder from the slums of New York. His gruff manner and hard personality hide the tender, vulnerable side of him. Rafe also possesses an insatiable thirst for knowledge that is a passion with him. Oddly enough, he has a wry sense of

humor that surfaces unexpectedly from time to time. And, though cynical to the extreme, he never lets his natural skepticism interfere with his innate sense of justice.

Heroine:
JANNA CANNON, a game warden for a small wildlife preserve, is a very dedicated lady. She is tall at five feet nine inches and carries herself in a stately way. Her long hair is dark brown and is usually twisted into a single thick braid in back. Of course, Rafe never lets her keep her hair braided when they make love! Janna is one quarter Cherokee Indian by heritage, and she possesses the dark eyes and skin of her ancestors.

Setting: Rafe's estate in Carmel, California

The Story:
Janna Cannon scaled the high walls of Rafe Santine's private estate, afraid of nothing and determined to appeal to the powerful man who could save her beloved animal preserve. She bewitched his guard dogs, then cast a spell of enchantment over him as well. Janna's profound grace, her caring nature, made the tough and proud Rafe grow mercurial in her presence. She offered him a gift he'd never risked reaching out for before—but could he trust his own emotions enough to open himself to her love?

Cover Scene:
In the gazebo overlooking the rugged cliffs at the edge of the Pacific Ocean, Rafe and Janna share a passionate moment together. The gazebo is made of redwood and the interior is small and cozy. Scarlet cushions cover the benches, and matching scarlet curtains hang from the eaves, caught back by tasseled sashes to permit the sea breeze to whip through the enclosure. Rafe is wearing black suede pants and a charcoal gray crew-neck sweater. Janna is wearing a safari-style khaki shirt-and-slacks outfit and suede desert boots. They embrace against the breathtaking backdrop of wild, crashing, white-crested waves pounding the rocks and cliffs below.

THE HOMETOWN HUNK CONTEST

CHARADE
(Originally Published as LOVESWEPT #74)
By Joan Elliott Pickart

COVER NOTES

The Characters:

Hero:
The phrase tall, dark, and handsome was coined to describe TENNES WHITNEY. His coal black hair reaches past his collar in back, and his fathomless steel gray eyes are framed by the kind of thick, dark lashes that a woman would kill to have. Darkly tanned, Tennes has a straight nose and a square chin, with—you guessed it!—a Kirk Douglas cleft. Tennes oozes masculinity and virility. He's a handsome son-of-a-gun!

Personality traits:
A shrewd, ruthless business tycoon, Tennes is a man of strength and principle. He's perfected the art of buying floundering companies and turning them around financially, then selling them at a profit. He possesses a sixth sense about business—in short, he's a winner! But there are two sides to his personality. Always in cool command, Tennes, who fears no man or challenge, is rendered emotionally vulnerable when faced with his elderly aunt's illness. His deep devotion to the woman who raised him clearly casts him as a warm, compassionate guy—not at all like the tough-as-nails executive image he presents. Leave it to heroine Whitney Jordan to discover the real man behind the complicated enigma.

Heroine:
WHITNEY JORDAN's russet-colored hair floats past her shoulders in glorious waves. Her emerald green eyes, full breasts, and long, slender legs—not to mention her peaches-

and-cream complexion—make her eye-poppingly attractive. How can Tennes resist the twenty-six-year-old beauty? And how can Whitney consider becoming serious with him? If their romance flourishes, she may end up being Whitney Whitney!

Setting: Los Angeles, California

The Story:
One moment writer Whitney Jordan was strolling the aisles of McNeil's Department Store, plotting the untimely demise of a soap opera heartthrob; the next, she was nearly knocked over by a real-life stunner who implored her to be his fiancée! The ailing little gray-haired aunt who'd raised him had one final wish, he said—to see her dear nephew Tennes married to the wonderful girl he'd described in his letters . . . only that girl hadn't existed—until now! Tennes promised the masquerade would last only through lunch, but Whitney gave such an inspired performance that Aunt Olive refused to let her go. And what began as a playful romantic deception grew more breathlessly real by the minute. . . .

Cover Scene:
Whitney's living room is bright and cheerful. The gray carpeting and blue sofa with green and blue throw pillows gives the apartment a cool but welcoming appearance. Sitting on the sofa next to Tennes, Whitney is wearing a black crepe dress that is simply cut but stunning. It is cut low over her breasts and held at the shoulders by thin straps. The skirt falls to her knees in soft folds and the bodice is nipped in at the waist with a matching belt. She has on black high heels, but prefers not to wear any jewelry to spoil the simplicity of the dress. Tennes is dressed in a black suit with a white silk shirt and a deep red tie.

THE HOMETOWN HUNK CONTEST

FOR THE LOVE OF SAMI
(Originally Published as LOVESWEPT #34)
By Fayrene Preston

COVER NOTES

Hero:
DANIEL PARKER-ST. JAMES is every woman's dream come
true. With glossy black hair and warm, reassuring blue
eyes, he makes our heroine melt with just a glance. Daniel's lean face is chiseled into assertive planes. His lips are
full and firmly sculptured, and his chin has the determined and arrogant thrust to it only a man who's sure of
himself can carry off. Daniel has a lot in common with
Clark Kent. Both wear glasses, and when Daniel removes
them to make love to Sami, she thinks he really is
Superman!

Personality traits:
Daniel Parker-St. James is one of the Twin Cities' most
respected attorneys. He's always in the news, either in the
society columns with his latest society lady, or on the
front page with his headline cases. He's brilliant and takes
on only the toughest cases—usually those that involve
millions of dollars. Daniel has a reputation for being a
deadly opponent in the courtroom. Because he's from a
socially prominent family and is a Harvard graduate, it's
expected that he'll run for the Senate one day. Distinguished-
looking and always distinctively dressed—he's fastidious
about his appearance—Daniel gives off an unassailable air
of authority and absolute control.

Heroine:
SAMUELINA (SAMI) ADKINSON is secretly a wealthy heiress. No one would guess. She lives in a converted ware-
house loft, dresses to suit no one but herself, and dabbles
in the creative arts. Sami is twenty-six years old, with

long, honey-colored hair. She wears soft, wispy bangs and has very thick brown lashes framing her golden eyes. Of medium height, Sami has to look up to gaze into Daniel's deep blue eyes.

Setting: St. Paul, Minnesota

The Story:
Unpredictable heiress Sami Adkinson had endeared herself to the most surprising people—from the bag ladies in the park she protected . . . to the mobster who appointed himself her guardian . . . to her exasperated but loving friends. Then Sami was arrested while demonstrating to save baby seals, and it took powerful attorney Daniel Parker-St. James to bail her out. Daniel was smitten, soon cherishing Sami and protecting her from her night fears. Sami reveled in his love—and resisted it too. And holding on to Sami, Daniel discovered, was like trying to hug quicksilver. . . .

Cover Scene:
The interior of Daniel's house is very grand and supremely formal, the decor sophisticated, refined, and quietly tasteful, just like Daniel himself. Rich traditional fabrics cover plush oversized custom sofas and Regency wing chairs. Queen Anne furniture is mixed with Chippendale and is subtly complemented with Oriental accent pieces. In the library, floor-to-ceiling bookcases filled with rare books provide the backdrop for Sami and Daniel's embrace. Sami is wearing a gold satin sheath gown. The dress has a high neckline, but in back is cut provocatively to the waist. Her jewels are exquisite. The necklace is made up of clusters of flowers created by large, flawless diamonds. From every cluster a huge, perfectly matched teardrop emerald hangs. The earrings are composed of an even larger flower cluster, and an equally huge teardrop-shaped emerald hangs from each one. Daniel is wearing a classic, elegant tuxedo.

LOVESWEPT® HOMETOWN HUNK CONTEST

OFFICIAL RULES

IN A CLASS BY ITSELF by Sandra Brown
FOR THE LOVE OF SAMI by Fayrene Preston
C.J.'S FATE by Kay Hooper
THE LADY AND THE UNICORN by Iris Johansen
CHARADE by Joan Elliott Pickart
DARLING OBSTACLES by Barbara Boswell

1. NO PURCHASE NECESSARY. Enter the HOMETOWN HUNK contest by completing the Official Entry Form below and enclosing a sharp color full-length photograph (easy to see details, with the photo being no smaller than 2½″ × 3½″) of the man you think perfectly represents one of the heroes from the above-listed books which are described in the accompanying Loveswept cover notes. Please be sure to fill out the Official Entry Form completely, and also be sure to clearly print on the back of the man's photograph the man's name, address, city, state, zip code, telephone number, date of birth, your name, address, city, state, zip code, telephone number, your relationship, if any, to the man (e.g. wife, girlfriend) as well as the title of the Loveswept book for which you are entering the man. If you do not have an Official Entry Form, you can print all of the required information on a 3″ × 5″ card and attach it to the photograph with all the necessary information printed on the back of the photograph as well. YOUR HERO MUST SIGN BOTH THE BACK OF THE OFFICIAL ENTRY FORM (OR 3″ × 5″ CARD) AND THE PHOTOGRAPH TO SIGNIFY HIS CONSENT TO BEING ENTERED IN THE CONTEST. Completed entries should be sent to:

BANTAM BOOKS
HOMETOWN HUNK CONTEST
Department CN
666 Fifth Avenue
New York, New York 10102–0023

All photographs and entries become the property of Bantam Books and will not be returned under any circumstances.

2. Six men will be chosen by the Loveswept authors as a HOMETOWN HUNK (one HUNK per Loveswept title). By entering the contest, each winner and each person who enters a winner agrees to abide by Bantam Books' rules and to be subject to Bantam Books' eligibility requirements. Each winning HUNK and each person who enters a winner will be required to sign all papers deemed necessary by Bantam Books before receiving any prize. Each winning HUNK will be flown via **United Airlines** from his closest United Airlines-serviced city to New York City and will stay at the ▪ll S꞉ɴɴɪᴛ Hotel—the ideal hotel for business or pleasure in midtown Manhattan—for two nights. Winning HUNKS' meals and hotel transfers will be provided by Bantam Books. Travel and hotel arrangements are made by *RELIABLE TRAVEL* and are subject to availability and to Bantam Books' date requirements. Each winning HUNK will pose with a female model at a photographer's studio for a photograph that will serve as the basis of a Loveswept front cover. Each winning HUNK will receive a $150.00 modeling fee. Each winning HUNK will be required to sign an Affidavit of Eligibility and Model's Release supplied by Bantam Books. (Approximate retail value of HOMETOWN HUNK'S PRIZE: $900.00). The six people who send in a winning HOMETOWN HUNK photograph that is used by Bantam will receive free for one year each, LOVESWEPT romance paperback books published by Bantam during that year. (Approximate retail value: $180.00.) Each person who submits a winning photograph

will also be required to sign an Affidavit of Eligibility and Promotional Release supplied by Bantam Books. All winning HUNKS' (as well as the people who submit the winning photographs) names, addresses, biographical data an l likenesses may be used by Bantam Books for publicity and promotional purposes without any additional compensation. There will be no prize substitutions or cash equivalents made.

3. All completed entries must be received by Bantam Books no later than September 15, 1988. Bantam Books is not responsible for lost or misdirected entries. The finalists will be selected by Loveswept editors and the six winning HOMETOWN HUNKS will be selected by the six authors of the participating Loveswept books. Winners will be selected on the basis of how closely the judges believe they reflect the descriptions of the books' heroes. Winners will be notified on or about October 31, 1988. If there are insufficient entries or if in the judges' opinions, no entry is suitable or adequately reflects the descriptions of the hero(s) in the book(s), Bantam may decide not to award a prize for the applicable book(s) and may reissue the book(s) at its discretion.

4. The contest is open to residents of the U.S. and Canada, except the Province of Quebec, and is void where prohibited by law. All federal and local regulations apply. Employees of Reliable Travel International, Inc., United Airlines, the Summit Hotel, and the Bantam Doubleday Dell Publishing Group, Inc., their subsidiaries and affiliates, and their immediate families are ineligible to enter.

5. For an extra copy of the Official Rules, the Official Entry Form, and the accompanying Loveswept cover notes, send your request and a self-addressed stamped envelope (Vermont and Washington State residents need not affix postage) before August 20, 1988 to the address listed in Paragraph 1 above.

LOVESWEPT® HOMETOWN HUNK OFFICIAL ENTRY FORM

BANTAM BOOKS
HOMETOWN HUNK CONTEST
Dept. CN
666 Fifth Avenue
New York, New York 10102–0023

HOMETOWN HUNK CONTEST

YOUR NAME_____

YOUR ADDRESS_____

CITY_____ STATE_____ ZIP_____

THE NAME OF THE LOVESWEPT BOOK FOR WHICH YOU ARE ENTERING THIS PHOTO

_____by_____

YOUR RELATIONSHIP TO YOUR HERO_____

YOUR HERO'S NAME_____

YOUR HERO'S ADDRESS_____

CITY_____ STATE_____ ZIP_____

YOUR HERO'S TELEPHONE #_____

YOUR HERO'S DATE OF BIRTH_____

YOUR HERO'S SIGNATURE CONSENTING TO HIS PHOTOGRAPH ENTRY

_____